The
BIRTHDAY GIRL

The
BIRTHDAY
GIRL

MELISSA DE LA CRUZ

DUTTON

DUTTON

An imprint of Penguin Random House LLC
penguinrandomhouse.com

Previously published as a Dutton hardcover in 2019
First trade paperback printing: July 2020

THE LIBRARY OF CONGRESS HAS CATALOGUED THE
HARDCOVER EDITION AS FOLLOWS:
Names: De la Cruz, Melissa, 1971–, author.
Title: The birthday girl : a novel / Melissa de la Cruz.
Description: New York : Dutton, [2019]
Identifiers: LCCN 2019010919 (print) | LCCN 2019012935 (ebook) |
ISBN 9781524743796 (ebook) | ISBN 9781524743772 (hc)
Subjects: | GSAFD: Mystery fiction.
Classification: LCC PS3604.E128 (ebook) | LCC PS3604.E128 B57 2019
(print) | DDC 813/.6—dc23
LC record available at https://lccn.loc.gov/2019010919

Dutton trade paperback ISBN: 9781524743789

Printed in the United States of America
1   3   5   7   9   10   8   6   4   2

BOOK DESIGN BY KATY RIEGEL

For Mike,
and for all my birthday girls
(and boys)

The
BIRTHDAY GIRL

Part One

FALSE STARTS

ONE

Last-Minute Preparations

October 19
The Present
5:00 P.M.

Ellie de Florent-Stinson had made a point of telling everyone she knew that she'd bought the house in Palm Springs for her birthday, as a *gift to self.*

Renting a Palm Springs house for a celebration was practically a rite of passage among a certain Los Angeles set, a flurry of Paperless Post invites with the requisite Rat-Pack-in-the-desert themes landing in one's inbox with a predictable thud over the years.

But Ellie always had to one-up, take it to the next mile, power it beyond the goalpost and smash it on the turf while doing an illegal victory dance—so she had actually *bought* a house, for a little over two million. Renting was so bourgeois.

Her phone had been blowing up with texts from excited friends for weeks.

Can't wait!!!

Me too!!

What should I bring??

Ellie snorted. This was no potluck. She texted, Yourself!

It was going to be perfect. Her fortieth birthday blowout at her new mid-century-modern pad that night was the pièce de résistance. She'd flown in the designer of her favorite Parisian hotels to turn a neighboring farm-to-table (or weeds-to-shithole as her husband joked) restaurant into a louche nineteenth-century Chinese opium den for the decadent after-*after*-party. (The *first* after-party would be held at the Ace Hotel's infamous Drag Queen Bingo bien sûr.) The designer had arrived the week before with real persimmons in tow (two euros each at the farmers market in Clignancourt) to hang from the newly bejeweled rafters. For the past two days, her guests had enjoyed guided spirit walks, hot yoga, mindfulness, tarot, and the Parker's two hot tubs. She'd flown in the majority of the motley crew from New York on Thursday night via YourJet, the semiprivate charter service app. The three-day event had been arranged down to every last detail—she'd even coerced a new acquaintance, a prize-winning novelist, to help write the children's loving speeches to her.

The party at her new home, Gulf House (so named because its original owner was said to have been the CEO of Gulfstream), was the icing on the cake, the cherry on the sundae, the culmination of a yearlong bacchanalian observance of the commencement of her fortieth year on the planet.

Except nothing was going the way she'd planned.

The hydrangeas were wilting and it was only five o'clock, an hour before her first guests were due to arrive. Fully half the flowers had died from exposure to the harsh desert climate. Of course it was Ellie's fault: She'd insisted on the fragile posies over the objections of her party planner and local florist, who had warned her that only sunflowers would be able to survive the desert heat. Ellie had nixed sunflowers as cheap, and so had to contend with the reality of the dead white blossoms. She wanted to scream, but instead texted Nathaniel, her long-suffering twentysomething assistant: THE!!! FLOWERS!! ARE!!! DYING!!!!! FIX IT!!!!!

Who knew October in Palm Springs would be as hot as Phoenix in July? Not Ellie. It was a goddamn one hundred ten degrees out, and even with the cloud of misters over the pool going at full blast, there was no denying it was as hot as Satan's armpit in the backyard. She took some consolation in the postcard-perfect golf course view, the sky a brilliant blue overhead. Plus, once the sun had set—four hours from now—it would be bearable. Right?

The house was situated in the south end of Palm Springs, in the old Canyon Country Club neighborhood, which was now called Indian Canyons because the land was leased from the tribe that owned it. Half the city sat on Native American land, hence the presence of casinos downtown. But Ellie insisted on calling it by its original name—the name of the country club when Frank Sinatra and Walt Disney used to golf there. If she'd been on the city council, she never would have allowed the name change. The older families bunkered down in the Vista Los Palmas neighborhood in the north end, which was supposedly more desirable because it wasn't leased land. But it was windy over there, and the views of the mountains were better on the south side of town. She'd fallen in love with her neighborhood's wide streets dotted with palm trees. Here in Indian Canyons, the homes weren't hidden behind high hedges or walls, so everyone could see exactly how fabulous your house was.

Ellie could have bought in the neighboring desert city of Rancho Mirage, in the swank confines of Thunderbird, where Gerald Ford famously retired and Barack and Michelle Obama were rumored to have bought a vacation home. But Rancho struck her as one gated community after another, soulless, moneyed, and contemporary, whereas Palm Springs proper had a certain old-fashioned cachet, a star-dusting of Hollywood history. The house was on a double corner lot and had practically a three-hundred-sixty-degree view of the golf course and the San Jacinto mountain range. She'd fallen in love the minute she walked through its double-height double doors painted in a cheery yellow, almost exactly three months ago.

"The second DJ is here," announced Lynn, her housekeeper from Los Angeles who'd agreed to work the weekend and who was plucking out dead hydrangeas from the floral arrangements and making them look lopsided. "Where should we put him?"

"In the game room," she replied.

"*Second* DJ?" asked her husband, Todd, walking into the terrazzo-floored living room and rolling his eyes. "Do we have *two* catering companies too? Or five? How many people are coming tonight anyway?"

"A bunch," she said airily. Ellie tried never to answer his questions directly. *How much was that handbag/bracelet/haircut/second house?* "A lot." *Where are you going?* "Out." *What time will you be home?* "Later."

They'd been in love, once. They even used to have sex—remember sex? Sure, married sex and all the lameness that phrase implied—hurried-before-the-kids-got-up or fatigued-after-the-kids-went-to-sleep kind of sex—but now she couldn't even remember the last time they'd done the deed. No wonder she was so uptight. It was ten years since that weekend in St. Barts when they'd pledged their trough—or was it *troth*? A trough was the thing pigs ate from, she thought. Although perhaps *trough* was the more appropriate word, now that Todd had gained fifty pounds after going on antianxiety, antidepression, anti-everything meds. Paging Todd's libido! Or maybe it wasn't the meds at all; just because he wasn't sleeping with *her* didn't mean he wasn't sleeping *around*, did it?

Did she even care if he was?

There they were, captured in that photograph in a silver frame resting on the piano. The four of them gathered near the shoreline: Todd—tall, dark-haired, as handsome as the former-actor-turned-laid-off-network-executive he was, snuggling his then eight-year-old daughter, Sam, the two of them looking adorable in matching white-on-white linen suits. They stood next to Ellie in her one-of-a-kind Alexandre Vauthier wedding gown flown direct from the designer's French atelier, the neckline falling off her bronze shoulder just so. It was the type of gown that should have rocked St. Paul's Cathedral to the awe of five hundred guests—ornate, ruffled, sequined, hand-sewn-by-blind-Belgian-nuns-type couture. Instead, Ellie had worn her long blond hair down and disheveled, looking like a goddess standing barefoot on that white sand beach, carrying baby Giggy in a matching lace sling. Their blended family was even more beautiful than a traditional one because you could read the hope and survival in Sam's mixed Chino-Anglo features, Todd's artfully unshaven chin, Giggy's quintessentially docile English baby face, and Ellie's defiant smile.

Now Todd was puffy in the face, red in the eye, sour in the disposition, less employed than he'd ever been, and possibly cheating on her; Sam, who'd always been her favorite, seemed to hate her guts; Giggy, who was ten years old, still couldn't read despite a quarter million dollars a year spent on private tutoring; six-year-old twins Elijah and Otis were surely causing their usual mayhem somewhere in the house; and Ellie's long-anticipated fortieth birthday party was teetering on disaster.

No matter, Ellie would get everything photoshopped to perfection later. Too bad there wasn't a Valencia filter to smooth out memories.

"Is Lord Fauntleroy coming?" Todd asked, using his favorite nickname for Giggy's biological dad.

"Of course Archer's coming," Ellie snapped. "You know that."

Ellie had invited everyone in her life to her fortieth birthday party in the same exact way that she'd invited everyone she knew—however barely—to her wedding ten years ago. She'd sent envelopes to the likes of Marc Jacobs, Karl Lagerfeld, and Anna Wintour. Privately, Ellie was a little embarrassed at her neediness, her graspy-ness, her *reach*.

But she couldn't help herself. She wanted more. She'd wanted desperately to be personal friends with Marc, Karl, and Anna, and even if all three had returned the response cards with polite regrets (carefully preserved in her wedding memory box), she was glad she'd tried. She'd had the sense not to invite them to her birthday party, instead focusing on the nouveau riche LA circle they ran in—parent friends from the kids' private schools, old friends from the garment trade in New York and London, a few boldfaced names from Todd's past, and rich couples they'd met at American Express Black Card events.

Of course she'd invited her first husband, Archer de Florent. It was only right since Giggy—*Imogen*—spent two weeks with him in London every year. Archer was almost twice Ellie's age, and at seventy-eight still wore his crisp bespoke white shirts unbuttoned down to his navel (to show off his year-round Caribbean tan) and tucked into his too-tight jeans. He'd surely be bringing one of his post-pubescent-looking girlfriends tonight. Artists, actresses, dreamers, and gold diggers all.

She'd been one of those girls once, sitting cross-legged on his yacht in a gold string bikini, all of seventeen, Archer smiling wolfishly from the captain's chair. They'd met on the circuit in St. Tropez.

Except instead of just a sore ass and a smile, Ellie had won the mother lode, so to speak, by securing the de Florent fortune. Back then, Archer couldn't wait to pop Ellie's cherry, couldn't believe he was so lucky, that he was her first (or so she'd told him), and he'd proposed and promised this gorgeous thing anything she wanted. She'd asked if she could give him a child once they were married, and he'd agreed. But before they tied the knot, they broke up a couple of times, finally marrying when she was twenty-two. She wanted a baby immediately, except the time was never quite right. Archer kept postponing it, and when she finally got pregnant, she was almost thirty and they were on the verge of divorce.

Ellie looked like she'd grown up in Connecticut hedge fund country and summered in Maine, with her thick flaxen hair (colored by the best, the same team that did Gwyneth's), a tiny, perfect nose (sculpted by the best, the same team that did actresses whose names can't be divulged), a deliberately crooked grin (flawed is more perfect than perfect because otherwise she'd look like a soap star—cheap), and golden tan, the kind of girl from whom American dreams were made. But in truth she was from a veritable trailer park, with a deadbeat dad and a scarred, world-weary mom in the withered branches of her family tree.

Not that Archer knew or cared about any of it, not when he'd married her, and not when they'd fucked in the penthouse suite of the Peninsula Hotel in Hong Kong to conceive Imogen. She'd forced his secretary to put it on his schedule and divert him from his meeting in Bahrain since Ellie was taking fertility drugs and ovulating. No matter that they were hardly speaking by then and hated each other's guts. He'd promised her a child and, boy, was he going to give her one.

Ellie had just finalized her divorce from Archer, and Giggy was four months old, when she met Todd, and for the first five years of her life, Todd was the only father Giggy ever knew. He'd wanted to give Giggy his last name even, and Ellie had considered it for a brief moment, but familial unity was no match for half the land in Norfolk, Beaumont Castle, and family history that went back to the sixth Earl of Surrey and a Viceroy of India—Archer's great-grandfathers, naturally. Imogen even had a title. Technically, she was Lady Imogen de Florent. Technically, Ellie had a title too, but she never used it; not even she would assume to reach that high. She wasn't a tacky Real Housewife.

Besides, six years ago, she and Todd had finally gotten their own little miracle. Two, to be exact. As if on cue, the twins ran in with jelly hands, sticky, fighting as usual.

"Eli! Otis! Stop that!" she yelled as they ran around the dining table, leaving handprints on the tablecloth.

She was turning forty, her company was worth thirty million dollars, she was "happily married" (a stretch, but they weren't getting divorced yet, so that was something), she had four gorgeous children (counting Sam, which she always did), and it was time to celebrate in this fabulous new house that she had bought fully furnished just two months ago.

It was going to be grand. Everyone who was everyone, everyone who mattered in her life, was going to be there tonight.

Her phone buzzed with yet another text. Assuming it was Nathaniel, her assistant, again, she started to type FUCK THE HYDRANGEAS GET ME SOME SUNFLOWERS when she saw the name on the screen.

Talk about a blast from the past.

From *before*.

Before she was Ellie de Florent-Stinson.

Before she was herself, really.

Happy birthday, girl.

The text came with a photo—taken twenty-four years ago. Sweet Sixteen, sigh. Could it really have been twenty-four years ago that she had been that young girl in that picture?

There she was, in all her glory. Her hair all over her face, her smile, wary instead of megawatt, her clothes, cheap and ill-fitting.

Another text: See you tonight.

A promise or a threat? Was she feeling butterflies or tasting bile? She looked at him in the photo, standing next to her, so handsome and so young.

It was her fortieth birthday. All the important people in her life would be there. Including *him*.

TWO

Bad Girls

October 19
Twenty-Four Years Ago
5:00 P.M.

Leo and Mish. Mish and Leo. They've been best friends since Leo came over to Mish's house and didn't say anything about how disgusting it was—dozens of unopened bills, yellowing leaflets and magazines piled on the coffee table, along with crusty coffee cups and empty beer cans brimming with cigarette butts, a ziggurat of catalogs and newspapers haphazardly piled against the walls, graveyards of dead potted plants, Mish's mom sitting on the couch, rolling a cigarette, not giving a shit about any of it. Leo didn't say a word, and Mish pretended not to care, even if they both knew Leo's mom would *never* let something like that stand. Even though they lived right next door in a similarly dilapidated trailer home, Leo's mom had dreams. Aspirations. She worked as a hostess at the nicer restaurant in the airport Ramada, and in the neighborhood, she was known as the uppity one, the one who acted like she didn't live there, the one who always left the house in an ironed blouse and her good pumps.

Portland was a pretty sleepy town, and not particularly snobby, but even so, there were people who had living rooms and people who didn't. No one who lived in Woods Forest Park, which was what the mobile home park was called, was at the living-room level. Leo often wondered what kind of moron came up with a name like Woods Forest anyway. Weren't they the same thing? The place had a dirty swimming pool, a coin-operated laundry where half the machines never worked, a basketball court where the local drug dealers did business, and a view of the polluted Columbia River. Leo's mom's life goal was to get them out of there as soon as possible. Their house was immaculate, even if it didn't have a living room. Meanwhile, Mish's mom had multiple tattoos and a rough voice and didn't own a vacuum.

Leo's mom had grown up on the bottom rung of the middle class, but her parents had died young, and there hadn't been enough money for college, plus she'd gotten pregnant in high school, and Leo's dad was in jail.

The rumor was that Leo's dad had killed someone with his fist. He'd gotten into an argument with a guy at the bus stop and clocked him good. One punch. Guy went down, hit the sidewalk at an unfortunate angle, and died immediately. It was an accident. Leo's dad hadn't meant to kill the guy, just, you know, punch him. Manslaughter. Leo's dad went away when Leo was a baby; Leo hardly knew him. Her mom had stopped visiting him a long time ago. Her parents might even be divorced, but it wasn't clear. Her mom didn't like to talk about him, and Leo learned not to ask too many questions.

It didn't matter. Mish's dad had gone to jail too, for dealing drugs, but he was out now. That was another thing they had in common—that their dads were felons.

Leo, everyone called her Leo, short for Eleanor, another of her mother's pretensions, people said. She was named Eleanor, for Eleanor of Aquitaine and Eleanor Roosevelt, and her mother had wanted people to call her Ella or Eleanor, but her dad called her Leo and it stuck. Leo was sixteen now; it was eight years since she'd gone over to Mish's house and looked at that disgusting mess of a home and, instead of being grossed out, decided she *liked* Mish, that they would be friends. Because Mish was cool.

Mish looked the same at sixteen as she did at eight, like a tiny, elfin waif, slightly feral and underweight; she never wore bras underneath her thin tank tops, and her nails were always colored in glitter, like shiny claws. She had her mother's narrow eyes and full lips, but no tattoos—yet.

In contrast, Leo always felt too big around Mish, like there was too much of her, like her hips were too wide and her hair was too coarse and too thick, even if it was the same exact shade as Mish's, the same platinum hue from the same cheap bottle. Leo felt like she took up way too much space, whereas Mish was a pixie; she looked like she existed on air and fumes.

School had started a few weeks ago, and they were still enrolled, unlike a few of the other kids who lived nearby. They were only sophomores by then, but already so bored. Leo's mom wanted Leo to go to college, but Leo's grades were terrible, so scholarships were out of the question. It was the reason they fought so much lately, with her mom asking her what she would do with her life, what did she think would happen. Leo didn't know. She thought she might model—don't laugh—because she'd been approached at the mall. Discovered. The lady had given her a card with a number. Lose twenty pounds and call me, she'd said.

Leo knew all about the "dangers of modeling," had watched the news shows and read all the warning articles in *Seventeen* and *Cosmo*. But this woman was middle-aged, frumpy like a schoolteacher, and firm. She seemed legit. Leo didn't tell Mish about it. Mish was getting an Icee from the lemonade and hot dog stand, the one where the girls (and it was always girls) wore tight red-white-and-blue striped uniforms with matching hats.

Leo kept the lady's card in her back pocket, like a talisman, like a lucky penny, like her ticket out. The lady said she was beautiful but *too big*, confirming everything Leo worried about privately. Lose the weight and call me. Leo told her mom to stop making so many mashed potatoes that same night.

School was a dead end. But maybe her looks would get her somewhere. *If* she could lose the weight. She wasn't at all fat, and was thinner than most girls already. But apparently not thin enough. It was depressing.

The girls were painting their nails together on Mish's couch. The couch smelled rank (the whole house smelled like unwashed laundry) but Leo didn't mind; it meant they could spill their Diet Cokes on the couch and no one would yell at them, or if she happened to shake the nail polish brush and a few little hot-pink flecks splattered on the plaid fabric, no one would notice.

Mish was painting her nails black, to match her lipstick. Mish was going through her goth phase. She looked like a dark fairy, with her bright hair against all the black she wore. Her current uniform consisted of a raggedy concert T-shirt and silk harem pants from Goodwill.

Meanwhile, Leo was just starting to get tired of looking like a reject, of wearing her outsider-y status on her sleeve. Her mother had even started buying her chinos from the Gap. Wanted her to look like the rich, preppy girls at school. Leo was starting to cave.

She brushed on the hot-pink polish. "It's my birthday, I feel festive," she said, finishing up her pinky toe and waving her feet in her friend's face.

"Ew!" said Mish, scrunching her nose.

It was Leo's birthday. Her mom was supposed to get out of work early so they could celebrate. Which meant a cheap Carvel cake and a twenty-five-dollar gift certificate to the Limited. But her mom would probably end up flaking like she always did. She wouldn't be able to get out early, they'd need her till midnight like always, and Leo would be stuck at home, alone, waiting, like every birthday before then. Leo was turning sixteen and wanted more than that. Just this once. Something to remember, to really mark the occasion, to make the day different from all the other days.

Other girls had Sweet Sixteen parties at the country club. Or at home, if they lived in one of those grand, historic Arlington Heights or Goose Hollow mansions with views of Mount Hood. Parties complete with waiters and DJs and all the popular kids driving their Beemers to the party. Those kids had everything they ever wanted handed to them and they still sucked. They were mean and insecure and stupid.

Leo had Mish.

And Mish was going to rise to the challenge. That's what friends were for.

The plan was to hit the mall, then . . . do something. Anything. Leo remembered the bottle of vodka that they'd been offered when it was passed around at the Madonna concert the other month. It was from the group in front of them, a couple of girls and a gay guy. The gay guy had really good eyeliner. Leo had never seen a guy wearing makeup before, except people on MTV like Robert Smith or Boy George, and at first she was a little scared of him. But he seemed harmless enough, and when he offered the vodka bottle, Mish took a slug.

Leo had shaken her head. She was too scared to drink something a stranger offered. She was wary of alcohol and what it did to her. Mish had raised her eyebrow in disgust. But then, Mish was the bad one. (The "badder" one.) They knew what people thought of them, poor girls from the trailer park; they knew what people expected from girls like them. Nothing. They were bad girls. They *looked* like bad girls. Maybe they were bad girls.

The group in front of them with the gay guy was friendly and asked if they wanted to go to IHop after, but Leo and Mish didn't have the money, so they said no. They had enough just to get to the concert; they couldn't afford to buy a T-shirt or any other souvenirs. The tickets were forty-five dollars each and they'd had to camp out in front of the Ticketmaster booth to get them. But then the gay guy had handed them the vodka bottle and told Leo to keep it, and even though just a tiny sliver of vodka was left, and even though she wouldn't even have a taste, it still felt like a present.

That's what Leo wanted tonight, something unexpected. A birthday surprise.

"Sweet sixteen," warbled Mish, putting away the nail polish bottle. "And never been kissed."

Leo laughed. "Never!"

"God, can you imagine?" said Mish. "To be so old and never been kissed? Like, what is wrong with you, then? Might as well never been fucked."

Leo shuddered. "Sad."

Mish had lost her virginity at thirteen. Mish knew things about boys. Knew how to sneak out of her bedroom window, knew how to give head. She'd shown Leo one day, demonstrating with a carrot. Leo had felt a little sick, watching. But that was Mish. Mish lived up to her reputation.

But then it happened to her too. One afternoon, when her mom was still at work, she lost her virginity, just like that. Leo thought there would be more to it, but it happened so quickly, and so out of the blue, that she almost thought it didn't count. At first, she didn't want to tell Mish about it, not at all, but then she freaked out when she didn't get her period for, like, five weeks, and she was sure she was pregnant and she had to tell someone.

Mish had screamed and hugged her. It was like they had accomplished something together. Maybe they had. What else did they have? They were terrible at everything else: sports, grades, art, whatever else other kids did; they didn't do those things. They weren't on a soccer or volleyball team and they weren't good at studying. This was what they did. They had sex with boys. Like

Madonna, whom they adored. She was the best of the bad girls. Like a bad girl saint.

And Leo wasn't pregnant, she'd just counted wrong, or lost track, or felt guilty about having sex while her mother was at work. But she was okay, she wasn't pregnant. Phew.

So the plan for Leo's birthday was to go to the mall and meet up with some guys. Mish had a boyfriend—she always did. She was dating Brooks Overton. Brooks was not goth. He was older, a popular senior, one of the rich kids, one of those boys with the shiny hair and perfect teeth who got up early for practice. Before Brooks and Mish started dating, he had been their joint crush. They shared a lot of things, and from sixth grade on, they'd shared an adoration of Brooks. It was common among the girls in their school. Everyone was in love with Brooks, even the moms. The moms were the worst, actually, making their worship too well known.

"Brooks!" Mrs. Richmond would coo from her Mercedes. "Look at you, you handsome boy, so grown up now!"

The other moms would titter, but it was clear they all got their panties wet for Brooks.

Brooks was Mish's boyfriend and no one liked it except Brooks and Mish. To their credit, Brooks's parents were cool about his trailer-park hoochie. They were lawyers, and this was Portland, not Boston. Brooks could date whomever he wanted, and he wanted Mish. Who wouldn't? The girl knew how to give head.

And if the cheerleaders and the honor students and the rich girls didn't like it, they didn't show it. Life wasn't *Pretty in Pink*. Maybe they didn't invite Mish to their parties or sleepovers or campouts. But they didn't say mean things to her face or make fun of her either. They just ignored her. If Brooks wanted to date her, he dated her alone. Brooks never hung out with his friends and Mish.

When Leo and Mish hung out with Brooks, they hung out with just the three of them, because god knows they didn't have any other friends at school. So they shared Brooks, even though Mish was the only one fucking him.

But since it was Leo's birthday, Brooks was going to bring some of his friends to meet them at the mall. To make it special. To make it different from all the other days.

Leo hoped the friends would be cute, even though no one was cuter than Brooks. She blew on her hot-pink nails. They looked good, like a pink Ferrari, flashy and racy. Sweet Sixteen and Never Been . . . what? Never Been Kissed? Nah. Sweet Sixteen and Never Been Loved. Listened to. Appreciated.

Sweet Sixteen and Never Been Fucked? Or Never Been Fucked Over?

"Stop with that thinking face," said Mish, who removed a Polaroid camera from her purse and waved it around. "To remember tonight forever!" She took a quick photo of Leo with her tongue sticking out.

"Ugh," said Leo. "I hate pictures!"

Mish ignored her as she put the photograph and her camera away. "Let's get to the mall. We need to celebrate!"

THREE

Last-Minute Cancellations

October 19
The Present
5:30 P.M.

Everything costs money; that's what her mom always used to say. Nothing was free in this world. Mo' money mo' problems; that was what P. Diddy used to say, or was it Biggie Smalls? Who was the one who died? Biggie? Tupac? Both? Ellie couldn't name a Tupac song to save her life and she didn't pay attention to rap battles but did try to keep abreast of the culture. You had to, especially if you were in the garment trade. Not that she liked the latest trends. It was annoying how all the hot new labels were these dirt cheap, ugly-as-sin clothes from Korean distributors who sold them through pretty girls' posts on Instagram. The kids who were buying them didn't care about labels anymore either; they were wearing twenty-dollar hoodies with nineties show logos (why was the *Friends* hoodie so popular with thirteen-year-olds? Was it Netflix? She'd have to ask Sam, who would know) and tiny T-shirts with aspirational or ironic quotes on them. It was the end of fashion.

Like every woman of her generation, Ellie would have died and gone to Chanel instead of heaven. She'd spent her first paycheck on a pair of those boots with the double-*C* clasp. It meant something, to wear Chanel. It meant you'd made it, that you had put your past squarely in the Kmart dustbin where it belonged. She wasn't sure if the kids who wore those new no-name labels cared about designers in the way that she and her friends used to. If they would kill to buy a Gucci bag like she did. Her own line, Wild & West, was meant for the hipster twenty- and thirtysomething, someone who wanted to look like she did, all flowing blond hair, barefoot and sexy in a sarong, but at their price point—five hundred dollars for a jersey jumpsuit—most of their clients were hot moms in their forties and fifties. She did a lot of business with a certain hard-bodied, suntanned, sun-bleached, second-wife type from the Laguna-Newport-Palm-Beach nexus.

She put away her phone and its disturbing text. She didn't have time to think about what that meant right now. Was *he* really coming? To the party? Could she stop him? Did she want to? Dammit! How did he even find out about it? She never posted on Facebook. (*Ew*, Facebook was for approval-seeking losers.) How did he even have her number? Someone must have given it to him. She shook her head and put those thoughts away.

There were so many things to do before her guests arrived. Make sure there were candles in the bathroom. Make sure they had the right fluffy paper towels out, the ones like they had at Barney's. *Thick. Soft.* You didn't want your guests using the same embroidered for-show-only guest towel, which would get bedraggled and gross by the end of the night. She'd learned that from her time with Archer. His penthouse had been stocked with all the right linens.

Then she had to make sure all the tealight votives were lit, the ones leading up to the driveway and the ones scattered all over the garden and by the pool. Make sure the pool candles were secured and ready to float. Put out the citronellas so they wouldn't be attacked by a thousand mosquitos when it got dark.

Another text.

I can't make it I'm so sorry. Happy birthday E xo M

From her oldest friend! They'd known each other forever, since they were kids. Ellie was annoyed. Who cancels a half hour before a party? Maybe she knew *he* was coming to the party. Maybe that was why Mishon wasn't showing up all of a sudden. It was weird to have a friend who knew you so well. Ellie wasn't even sure she liked it, or if she kept her around because she knew all her secrets. Well, almost all of them.

Todd huffed by her; her husband always got anxious before every social gathering, and parties at their house brought out the worst. He was snapping at the caterer, growling at the bartenders, yelling at the kids. She should be used to it by now, but mostly it was irritating. Just take a fucking Xanax and relax already. He wasn't even dressed—he was still wearing a ratty T-shirt and board shorts.

"Don't put that there!" he yelled at a hapless waiter who had moved one of the vases from the mantel to make room for a line of shot glasses. "It'll stain the wood!"

The waiter startled and almost dropped the vase.

"Todd!" Ellie said, hands on hips.

He wheeled toward her, looking positively murderous. "What?"

"STOP IT!"

"STOP WHAT?"

It was her birthday. For one day out of the fucking year, could he not be himself for once? One day. One night. To celebrate herself and her achievements, couldn't he just let them have a nice party? She promised herself she wouldn't fall for it, that she would let him rant and rage because when the doorbell rang and the first guest arrived, he always turned into the consummate host, pressing drinks and making small talk and making everyone feel so warm and welcome. He was good at that. But for the hour before the party, he was awful.

So it always happened that Todd was smooth and smiling when the guests arrived, while Ellie would be the one shaken and brittle because they had just had a screaming fight in front of all the help beforehand.

Don't do it, don't do it, she told herself.

She did it.

"FUCKING GET OUT OF THE WAY ALREADY AND LET THESE PEOPLE DO THEIR FUCKING JOBS!" she screamed at him.

"FUCK YOU! DON'T FUCKING TELL ME WHAT THE FUCK I CAN DO IN MY OWN FUCKING HOUSE!" he screamed back.

The caterer ignored them; she'd seen it all before.

Todd stomped away, having dumped all his social anxiety on

his wife, who was now, predictably, shaken and brittle and full of rage.

Why? Why was she even having this party anyway? It wasn't for fun. It was to show off. To let everyone gawk at the yards of diamonds dripping down her cleavage in her new straight-from-the-runway Delpozo dress and to wear her new Lucite heels from that tranny boutique downtown. Yeah, she still said *tranny*; she knew you weren't supposed to say it anymore, which was why she said it. Tranny. You were supposed to say *transgender* or *gender-queer* like Sam's friends, all those beautiful boy-girls and girl-boys. But what else would you call a store that sold seven-inch heels up to size fifteen, a store that was practically *exploding* with marabou feathers?

The doorbell rang, and since Ellie was the closest one to it, she opened it, annoyed that someone had arrived early. Didn't people know it was a faux pas to arrive early to a party? When the invite said six o'clock, it meant please arrive at six thirty. Any earlier was simply irritating and provincial.

But it wasn't a guest standing at the doorway, it was Sam.

Samantha Alyson Stinson. Her stepdaughter.

"Sam!" she said. "What are you doing here? You're not supposed to be home till Thanksgiving! And look at your hair!"

Sam had cut her hair. It was very, very short, almost like a crew cut. Did this mean she was also going through a gender-fluid phase?

"I dyed it blond and hated it, so I had to cut it because it was falling out," said Sam. So no, not a sexual orientation signifier but a hair fail.

Ellie put her arms around her kid. Sam was her kid as much as

Giggy and Otis and Eli. Maybe she even loved Sam more because she didn't want to love her any less. Didn't want to be pegged as *that* stepmom. "You're too skinny!"

"Is the party tonight?" Sam asked, scowling at the flurry of activity around the house. "Oh, fuck."

"Wait, you didn't come home for my party? This isn't a surprise you and Daddy cooked up? And don't swear; it's tacky," she admonished.

Sam sighed. "No, Ellie, it's not."

Ellie wished Sam would call her Mom, or Mommy, or Mama, like she used to, when she was a kid. But lately, Sam called her by her first name, which was annoying. She supposed it was because technically Sam already had a mom. Montserrat was invited to the party even. It was a magnanimous gesture on Ellie's part, given all the toxic history between Montserrat and Todd, Montserrat and Ellie, Montserrat and the three of them, Montserrat who had a habit of calling child services on Ellie and Todd, Montserrat who had made Sam believe that Ellie had stolen her father from them, Montserrat who had overdosed twice and, once when Sam was just twelve, locked her out of the house at three in the morning after throwing a water bottle at Sam's head (ouch), but of course when the police officers came, they'd questioned Todd. Ellie had been in China, at the factory, haggling with her suppliers in the middle of a big meeting when she got a call from her hysterical child saying Montserrat had freaked out and she was alone, on the street, at three A.M., please come get her.

But of course now Montserrat (stupid name) was Mom, Montserrat was sober, Montserrat was a life coach (of all things!). And

Ellie was just Ellie. Not the parent who had flown out that very hour from Shenzhen to deal with the mess. Not Mom. No! Not that. Just Ellie.

Sam put her dusty bags down on the terrazzo. "I don't want to talk about it."

"Why not?"

Sam raised her eyebrow. She looked like a cute baby lesbian, like Jenny Shimizu, Angelina Jolie's Japanese model girlfriend before she married and divorced Brad Pitt and became Mother Teresa slash Mia Farrow with all those children. Ellie decided it was kind of a good look on Sam. Asian butch girl. Maybe she would put Sam in the latest Wild & West campaign.

"Because there's nothing to say," said Sam in a belligerent tone.

Ellie sighed. Todd was supposed to be dealing with Sam, and to be on top of whatever problems she had. Sam's issues—academic, emotional, and otherwise—were supposed to be more his responsibility than hers, since she was his biological child. At least he was supposed to be on it while Ellie was trying to fix the financial mess they were in. But of course Todd had dropped the ball. Ellie did not have the bandwidth to deal with whatever this was right now. *Right now*, she was in the middle of selling her company to a wealthy Korean investor (if you can't beat them, join them, or in her case, sell fifty percent to them) and trying to keep everything afloat and one step ahead of the bill collectors.

Besides, Sam had never been much trouble. The kid had always been a straight-A-plus nerd. She never had any friends, had withdrawn into herself and her studies as a rebellion against her hard-partying cokehead mom and her negligent dad and her too-busy-at-work stepmom. Ellie had done her best. And she considered Sam a fait accompli.

Sam was at Stanford! It was something Ellie dropped into every conversation. *We can't make it to dinner because we're visiting our eldest at Stanford. Stanford homecoming is next week! Stanford housing is so expensive! We can't decide whether to fly or drive down to Stanford. Stanford, Stanford, Stanford*; it was a mantra to keep bad luck, bad fortune, bad things from happening. It was a sign that they'd done well by their kids, that they were the best parents in the world. Stanford! They'd made it all the way to the top! Take that, child services!

"Did something happen at school?" asked Ellie.

Sam shrugged and took out her phone, started texting someone.

Ellie took a deep, calming breath. "Fine. Have it your way. We'll talk about this later. Get ready for the party. You look like you just got out of a plane."

"Thanks, Mom."

Against her better judgment, knowing full well the kid was just manipulating her, trying to get on her good side, Ellie felt herself melt at being called Mom again.

"Okay, go! Hurry! The guests will be here any minute!"

Sam went, and the doorbell rang again.

FOUR

Mall Rats

October 19
Twenty-Four Years Ago
5:30 P.M.

Since it was Leo's birthday, they were going to Washington Square, the good mall all the way out in Tigard, not the one just five minutes away. The good mall had the better shops. It was shiny, clean, and had recently been renovated. The mall nearby was old. It had a Sears and a JC Penney, and a Casual Corner, which even her mom found too frumpy. If they were feeling cheesy, they went to Merry-Go-Round, but mostly they ended up at Mervyn's, which was like Sears but just a tiny bit nicer (no power tools), though nothing like the Nordstrom at the good mall. Mish called it "the Nordstrom's," which annoyed Leo because there wasn't a Mr. Nordstrom or a Nordstrom family who owned it (she didn't think), plus it sounded so . . . *uneducated*. The plan was to head to Brass Plum to shop(lift) and then meet the boys at the food court.

Leo wanted to put the nail polish away in her bureau, so they walked across the alley to her house. Mish waited by the front door. Leo grabbed her backpack and checked her lipstick in the mirror, and as she walked out of the room, she tripped on the loose tile by the doorway, almost falling on her ass.

"Walk much?" smirked Mish.

Leo colored. The tile had been broken for months now, and while her mother kept a neat house, she didn't know anything about maintenance or larger repairs. There were broken blinds in almost all the windows, cracks in the ceiling, and mold in the bathroom. Tidying up wasn't enough.

"You guys should really take care of that," said Mish. "I know some guy who fell and hit his head on the sidewalk and he *died*."

"Yeah, because my dad *killed* him," said Leo, who didn't find it funny.

"It was an accident!" said Mish, who always found the story fascinating. That someone could die from a punch, from a fall. That was all it took.

"Shut up," said Leo, grabbing a key to the house on their way out.

Neither of them had cars, even though Mish had a driver's license, so they took the bus. Walking over to the stop, there was a slight mist in the air, and Leo worried her hair would pouf up. It was gray out, but then, it was always gray out. That was the problem with living in the Pacific Northwest; the sky was slate, never blue. It was always about to rain, or had just stopped raining, or raining. Leo was sick of rain.

It was embarrassing to wait at the curb with all the old people and the poor people and the old and poor people carrying plastic sacks. No one else they knew took the bus. Leo wished Brooks had offered to pick them up, but even Mish didn't want him to see where they lived. The reality of their circumstances was too far from what he was used to. Leo had been in Brooks's house a few times, had gawked at the large pantry filled with snacks from Costco and the fact that his family subscribed to all the cable channels. That's what impressed her the most. The height of wealth was signified by unlimited TV and corn chips more than the formal dining room or the chrome-and-glass tables in the living room, with the weirdly shaped pastel vases that Mish explained were "artistic."

When they'd hung out at Brooks's, Mish had been right at home, pouring orange juice into glasses and acting like a host. Brooks held up the remote and flicked over to MTV. Leo had sat at the edge of the couch, not even daring to lean back. But as the afternoon wore on, and they played a few hands of War, and Mish spilled a whole bowl of popcorn on the rug and Brooks only laughed, Leo had been able to relax a little. She'd told her mom about every detail of the house, about the pretty planters by the window and the fact that they had a room devoted just to watching TV. It was off the kitchen, and when Brooks was little, it had been his playroom. The shelves were still stacked with plastic bins full of Legos.

If Leo wished for a moment that there was going to be a surprise birthday party for her in that large, comfortable house later that day, she would never admit it to Mish. It was just a fantasy, a sweet daydream. There was no way that would ever happen. Mish would never even dream of asking Brooks. Mish's own birthday was a few days later, and even then, there were no plans to celebrate at Brooks's house.

The bus came, finally, groaning to a stop and making a hissing noise as it crouched down to let the elderly passengers up. Leo and Mish waited their turn, and Leo fished around in her pocket for her quarter. "Transfer, please," she told the bus driver, who handed her a blue ticket she could use to get back home.

"We don't need a transfer. I'm sure we can get a ride later," said Mish.

"Really?" asked Leo. "From whom?"

"Arnold said he'd try to meet up with us later maybe," said Mish. Arnold was a guy from their neighborhood, something of a big-brother type. He kept an eye out for them, which was sweet, until you remembered he was also basically a dropout and a drug dealer.

"Um, okay," said Leo. She took the transfer anyway. You never knew. Arnold could be flaky.

And Mish tended to overpromise; she couldn't help it. It was her way, like with the homecoming dance just a few weeks ago. She'd told Leo that she *had* to come with them, that she and Brooks were all going in a huge group. Leo didn't even need a date, Mish said; some people were going stag. The point was to just go together and have fun. Leo had never been to homecoming before, neither the game nor the dance after. But Mish had insisted she "come with." And so Leo made her mom sew her a dress that she could wear. They found a pattern for a tight black sheath. But then the weeks passed and when Leo would ask Mish about specific plans, like where were they all meeting and whom she could ride with, Mish would just wave her away or say, "Um, I dunno, let me find out . . ."

But she never did. Homecoming week came and went. Maybe Mish forgot about inviting Leo. Or maybe she was too embarrassed to bring her along to one of the rare outings with a larger group of Brooks's friends. Or maybe she changed her mind and didn't want Leo there. Leo put the dress away. Maybe she'd wear it some other time. Mish went to homecoming. Leo saw the photos on her desk one afternoon, but she never confronted Mish about it. She didn't even ask Mish how it went. It was one of those things that was just left unsaid between them. Supposedly, Brooks got crowned homecoming king and Stacey Anders was queen. Stacey was probably the most popular girl in school, pretty, rich, a cheerleader but also a member of Students against Drunk Driving and the debate team, headed for Dartmouth.

Leo and Mish found seats in the back of the bus, and Leo took the window seat. The mist hugged the tops of the fir trees, and she could see the bay not too far away. Mish put on her headphones and chewed her gum and zoned out. Leo could hear the tinny music from her Walkman. The Cure, it sounded like.

That was what was nice about having a best friend—they didn't have to talk to each other all the time. If Mish might be a little smug about her handsome Arlington boyfriend, well, wouldn't any girl be the same?

Mish didn't know what would come next, though. Leo's mother always told her what was in store for girls like Mish: pregnancy, her own trailer, and another deadbeat boyfriend. Brooks was never going to marry a girl like Mish. She was just his high school hookup, the local tramp he'd talk about in wonder and a little pride to his future wife, some Stacey Anders type, who'd raise their 2.5 children in their perfect home with their perfect life until the cycle repeated itself all over again and his perfect son ended up at Arlington High. Just like Mish would repeat her mother's cycle. Maybe their kids would even date, ha.

That's why Leo wanted out, she didn't want any part of that, and if she had to do it all on her own, she would. Somehow, she would. She was only sixteen years old, but she already knew her dreams were too big for this stupid little town. She sat in silence and looked out at the view. One day, she would leave this place and never come back. She didn't aspire just to a better neighborhood. She wanted out of the state even. Out of the West Coast, maybe even out of America.

"Oh, hey, you're Leo, right?" Leo looked up to see a girl from school standing in front of her. It was Shona Silverstein. Leo was surprised to see her on the bus. "Hey, M," Shona said to Mish.

Mish removed her headphones delicately and gave Shona a sweet smile. "Hi, girl, what are you doing on the Green Beast?"

Shona explained she took the bus when her older brother had to stay late for band. She was awfully friendly to Mish, and Leo got the impression that while the girls knew each other through Brooks, and that Shona was maybe part of that "big group" that had gone to homecoming together, Mish was closer to that group of girls, and particularly Shona, than she had ever let on before. Mish explained what they were doing.

"Oh, it's your birthday too? Happy birthday!" said Shona,

turning to Leo and clapping her hands as if delighted. Leo wondered why she cared. And what did she mean by "it's your birthday too"? Who else had a birthday today?

"We're going shopping, then meeting the guys," said Mish.

Shona raised her eyebrows approvingly. "You guys should come to Stace's party. I mean, if you have nothing to do later. Not that you don't, but you know, you should stop by."

"Sure, maybe," Leo said. Why was Shona being so nice? Was it because Mish was part of the group now? In any event, Leo was definitely still a hanger-on, if that.

Shona got off at her stop, by the entrance to one of those hilly neighborhoods. Several tired-looking women, nannies and housekeepers most likely, got on the bus when she left.

Before Mish put her headphones back on, Leo elbowed her. "Let's go to the party."

"At Stacey's? Why?" Mish made a face.

"Isn't Brooks friends with all those guys?" said Leo. She was heading dangerously into the unsaid territory between them, but she forged on. "I mean, don't *you* hang out with them?"

Mish shrugged. "Sort of. But they're all seniors and all they talk about is college." She rolled her eyes. "I'm, like, this idiot, and they're all so fucking smart it's annoying. Doesn't matter. All Brooks cares about is making out."

"Um, gross," said Leo, cracking up.

Mish made kissy-faces and noises and they laughed even harder. It was difficult to hold grudges against a friend like that.

They arrived at the mall and had to walk the length of the parking lot to get to the entrance, trudging through the rain. It was deliciously warm and smelled like cinnamon rolls once they got inside. Leo felt a little self-conscious in her old parka and combat boots. Like she had POOR stamped on her forehead. Her hair had frizzed and they didn't have umbrellas, so they probably looked like two wet dogs. Mish laughed as she shook out her hair and droplets fell on the marble floor. "It's your birthday!" she squealed, jumping up in the air. "YOUR BIRTHDAY!!!"

People turned around and stared. Mish was always making a spectacle of herself. Wanted people to notice her. Leo pulled her down mid-jump. "STOP!" she said, laughing. "SHUT UP! OH MY GOD! You're crazy!"

"I'm CRAZY FOR YOU!!!" Mish yelled. Her cheeks were bright pink and she really was so pretty and doll-like. No wonder Brooks had chosen her. She grabbed Leo's hand and they ran through all the cheerful stay-at-home moms in their puffer vests and white button-downs, holding Williams-Sonoma shopping bags, their daughters in rugby shirts and pristine white Tretorn sneakers.

They stared at the two wet girls.

But for once, Leo didn't care. Mish's joy was infectious, and it was a kind of defiant, dare-you-to-tell-us-to-shut-up kind of joy, because no matter what, they knew that the crowd was also staring at them because they were young, and they were beautiful, glittering, maybe even the most beautiful they would ever be, at this moment, rain-wet and makeup-running as they hoofed it to the store.

FIVE

Early Arrivals

October 19
The Present
6:00 P.M.

The doorbell rang again, and when Ellie opened the door, she decided to keep it unlatched so that the next guests would be able to saunter inside without having to wait. She usually did that for a party, but the fight with Todd, plus Sam's unexpected arrival, had thrown her off her game. Why was Sam here? School had just started. Something *must* have happened at school. She hoped it wasn't anything too disastrous; Sam tended to be overdramatic and sensitive. Just like her mother, Ellie couldn't help but think, having little patience for the self-pitying drama both Montserrat and Sam created. She was forever telling her kids to "buck up" or her husband to "man up" or her employees to "just fucking deal with it already!"

After all, look at her. She came from nothing to forge this amazing life they had. If she could do it, anyone could. Todd always complained she had no sympathy for weakness or vulnerability, and he was right about that. She had survived the apocalypse that was her childhood to live in paradise. Why couldn't everyone else do the same, when their lives were so much softer than hers used to be?

Anyway, her assistant, Nathaniel, was late as usual (she'd forgotten she'd sent him to get sunflowers), and so there was no one to open the door and take the ladies' purses and put them away in the coat closet, or take the proffered hostess and/or birthday gifts and display them on the gift table. She tried to force her face into a friendly smile and opened the door with a flourish.

"DARLING!" Sterling Burwell bellowed. He was her best friend in Palm Springs, the guy who'd found and sold her this house. Her realtor. He was dressed in a white suit with a lavender shirt and pocket square, and his voice had the rich, dulcet tones of the mayor of a small Southern (*Suhthun*) town in Virginia, which is where he was from. Ellie, who had only been to Miami and otherwise avoided the South, once asked him if he was from an old Yankee family, and Sterling had reeled. He'd put a hand to his heart and, with his most patrician accent, explained that he was from *Vuh-ginny-yuh*, and his family roots went back further than those arrivistes from the *Mayflower*.

"HAPPY BIRTHDAY, DOLL!" he said, giving her a dramatic double-cheek air-kiss and presenting a jeroboam of champagne. "Don't drink it all at once, or maybe we should," he giggled.

"Thank god it's just you," she said, staggering under the weight of the giant bottle. "I was worried it was a guest."

Sterling didn't seem to mind the almost-insult and began to inspect the house while she handed off the gift to one of the cater-waiters.

"You got rid of the Liberace chandeliers," he said, looking up at the simple Jasper Morrison Glo-Balls her contractor had hastily installed in the entrance hall ceiling just last week. "Good choice."

"Yeah, we ditched the infinity mirrors too. I mean, right? It's not Versailles." She would save Versailles for her fiftieth, she promised. Private party in the ballroom, duh!

Sterling fanned himself with the birthday card he'd brought. He was in his late seventies, a "young buck" according to, well, himself. ("You know what they say. It's the gay nineties in Palm Springs; everyone's gay and ninety.")

When Ellie thought of Palm Springs, she thought of Coachella, the music festival held every spring just a few miles away, of starlets in crochet bikini tops and short shorts, making peace signs and wearing flower crowns. Palm Springs meant hipsters on mopeds heading to the Ace Hotel to drink tiki cocktails. Palm Springs was young, and hip, and cool. Or so the marketing for the new hotels downtown wanted you to believe.

Sterling was a throwback. A dying breed. (Pun definitely intended.) Ellie was starting to suspect there were more of them—gay retirees—than she was first led to believe. She and Todd had had several dinners at the country club across the way, packing the kids in the golf cart and zooming across the trails, and everyone there was geriatric. Ancient as the menu, which served oysters Rockefeller and steak Diane. Ten-year-old Giggy asked if there were any vegan entrées and the waiter had just looked confused.

This whole desert adventure was unraveling, just like when they bought the house in Park City a few years ago because it seemed like such a fun, buzzy town. There were parties every night and the bars were packed. Turned out it was only that way because they were there during Sundance. The rest of the time, it was a sleepy hamlet full of Mormons who skied. Had she made the same mistake buying this white elephant in the desert?

Sterling had introduced her to all the aging celebrities, aka "the stars of yesteryear," who lived in her neighborhood, including Barry Manilow and Suzanne Somers. They were both invited tonight, of course. Ellie would much rather have had Sofia Coppola and Leonardo DiCaprio, but apparently, Sofia had sold her Palm Springs house years ago (who knew?) and Leo was at the Venice Film Festival. Not that she knew Leo. But still. Supposedly, Anne Hathaway had just bought a house in the desert, or was it Jennifer Aniston? Barack and Michelle were supposed to have bought that house in Rancho Mirage, but no one ever saw them anywhere. And god knows Ellie had *tried*.

"Where's Howie?" she asked, meaning Sterling's husband, who was a mortgage broker and a spry sixty-eight.

"He's coming later," he said dismissively, waltzing up to the outdoor bar and eyeing the handsome bartender. "What's yummy other than you?"

"Uh, Sterling, stop. Leave the boy alone," she said, pursing her lips in a frown. She made a conciliatory gesture to Victor, a young Australian actor whom they hired to work all their parties. He'd once been on a show Todd had green-lit, but when *Castmembers!* was canceled after one season, he needed to supplement his income. In all honesty, the man could not craft a decent cocktail to save his life—they were either way too strong or far too sweet, and never quite right—but nevertheless everyone adored him. Beauty went far (she should know), and more often than not, they would find Victor downing shots and taking selfies with the guests. He often posted photos from their parties on his social media and drank as much as anyone at the party.

"All good, mate," said Victor, giving the cocktail jug a good shake. "We've got a forty-deuce and a cuarenta caliente," he said. "Basically, a cosmopolitan with white raspberry juice and a 'skinny' margarita."

"White cranberry juice?" asked Sterling.

"No colored drinks!" Ellie explained, motioning to the snow-white Minotti couch that took up two walls in the living room.

Sterling nodded in approval. "I'll just have a vodka on the rocks. You have Tito's?" Of course they did.

"The usual for me, Vic," she said.

They were served. Sterling's pinky pointed up in the air as he raised his drink to his lips. "The flowers are wilting."

"Tell me about it," she said, taking a sip from her own cocktail. She suppressed a grimace. Way too strong, as usual.

"Not your fault. Lordy, it is hot."

"But dry," she reminded him, which was something the good citizens of Palm Springs said to each other all the time. That it wasn't so terrible since it was a dry heat. Sure, like being roasted slowly in the oven. Make sure it's a Viking.

"As dry as a . . ." began Sterling. But before he could finish his metaphor, Todd joined them, suave and friendly. He'd showered and changed and was wearing a crisp white Oxford and the linen pants she'd bought him from Italy last year. He gave Sterling a hug and Sterling beamed. That was one good thing about Todd;

he liked her friends. What other wife could say the same of her husband? As much as they fought, they also socialized together. She never went anywhere without him if she could help it.

The three of them walked over to the edge of the pool overlooking the golf course, the San Jacinto Mountains turning pink in the sunset. With cocktails in hand and Sterling's jaunty attire, they made a tableau similar to the Slim Aarons photograph of a poolside party at the Kaufmann house, which was hanging in the family room. From across the way, they could see the fountains of the golf club, catching the light just so and creating a rainbow. Ellie took another glug of her vodka martini. It was growing on her. So what if it was too strong. It was also ice-cold and salty, just the way she liked it.

Yeah, it was hot. What did you expect? It was the desert. She was content, maybe even happy. Sterling always put her in a good mood. Especially now that they were having cocktails and she was over the fight with Todd. It was just nerves. The weekend had been a success so far. This was forty. This was as good as it ever got. The photographer from *Vanity Fair* was supposed to arrive later. She hoped her makeup would hold.

"So how's business?" Todd asked, a hand in his pocket. "This house going to hold its value?"

Sterling chuckled. "You guys got a great deal. No one buys in Palm Springs in August."

"Only my wife," said Todd, and for a moment they were dangerously close to bickering again, but Ellie chose to let it go.

"Listen to the man, we got a bargain!" she hooted.

"When *do* they buy in the desert?" Todd asked, curious.

"November to May mostly. High season. They get out here, it's January, and eighty degrees, and everywhere else it's below zero. I almost can't keep up with demand. But then summer comes and it scares everyone away."

Like most of their neighbors, Sterling and Howie lived in the desert only part-time. During the low season, they absconded to their home in Hawaii. Ellie pictured a cute modern tree house in Honolulu; they seemed the type. When they weren't in the islands or in the desert, they traveled extensively, Ellie knew, because she'd been in their house several times, and in the den, there was a framed map of the world with pushpins, and every pushpin was a place they had been. At the top of the map, someone had scrawled in capital letters: *STERLING AND HOWIE'S EXCELLENT ADVENTURES!* Ellie had tried not to cringe, but she supposed cheesiness came with age. When she and Todd were that old and creaky, they'd probably do the same. Except hers would read *WHERE IN THE WORLD ARE ELLIE AND TODD?!*

They continued to admire the sunset, which never failed to please, all glorious scarlet and gold hues over the mountains, although Ellie preferred the sunrise, the softer pink of dawn, which greeted her from her east-facing bedroom.

"You know why Palm Springs became so popular with Hollywood, don't you?" asked Sterling. They shook their heads. "The studios used to have a clause that the actors couldn't be farther away than eighty miles at all times. They had to be able to get on set if needed. And Palm Springs was just exactly eighty miles away, so it was a perfect getaway."

That led to the usual Palm Springs chitchat, about how Clark

Gable's old house was now a restaurant, and how Frank Sinatra's old estate—complete with his old recording studio—was available for rent. Sterling told them about how Bob Hope and his family used to move his entire court out to the desert during the high season, traveling like King Louis from Paris to Versailles, with all their servants and their china. The Hope caravan heralded the season of golf and parties. Ellie nodded; she'd seen the photos— of Nancy and Ronald Reagan, Betsy Bloomingdale, all the old eighties icons yukking it up.

The city had a storied and glamorous past, but Ellie didn't want to live in the past, she wanted it to matter now, and it was one of those things she and Todd constantly argued about. Whether they—or she, since she had bought the house without consulting him—had made a mistake by buying out here. What if they had been sold an empty bill of goods? What if the only people who came out here were dying? They couldn't make another bad investment.

"Remember, when you sell it, call me," said Sterling. "I've flipped a dozen of these."

"Good, we just might," said Todd meaningfully, catching her eye.

"Honey!" said Ellie. "We just bought the house. Can't we enjoy it first?"

"If we can afford it," said Todd grumpily.

Ellie rolled her eyes at him and there was a strained silence that Sterling pretended not to notice. "Where is everyone?" he asked, looking around and realizing he was the only one at the party who wasn't working it other than the hosts.

"The party bus is picking up people from the Parker around

now," Ellie explained. "They should be here soon. Then everyone else is driving over or Ubering, I guess."

But the happy buzz she'd felt at her first sip of alcohol had dissipated with Todd's insistence on bringing up money and investments. It sent a cold shiver down her spine. Couldn't he talk about something else? Couldn't she have one night when they didn't have to worry about the bills?

She just wanted to have this. One night. But since he'd broached the topic of money, she could exact revenge by needling him about his daughter. "You spoke to Sam, right?" she asked, assuming that of course Todd had seen his daughter had arrived for the party.

"Sam's home? I didn't see her!" said Todd. "How'd she even know we were out here and not in LA?"

"I don't know. I thought she came home as a surprise for my birthday, that you two had cooked it up," said Ellie. "But that's okay, she told me it wasn't that."

Todd looked flustered. "Oh, ah, well . . ."

Ellie sighed. It's not like she expected her husband to try to do nice things for her; it's just that he never did. Like it seriously didn't occur to him that it might be nice for the whole family to be together for her fortieth?

"I mean, she's busy at school," said Todd defensively. "And it seemed like this party was for your friends."

"*My* friends? What does that mean?" asked Ellie, annoyed. If they were only *her* friends, then it was sad, for it meant Todd didn't have any friends of his own.

"Nothing," he said tersely. "Drop it."

"It's fine," she said dismissively. "Well, she's here now."

"Why?"

"I don't know; she won't tell me."

"I'll talk to her," he said grimly.

"You do that," she said through gritted teeth, her goodwill toward Todd now completely gone.

They eyed each other warily, then Todd shrugged, as if he didn't have the energy for another fight. "Come on, Sterling, let me show you what we did with the bathrooms," he said, heading toward the sliding door.

"You already remodeled the bathrooms?"

"You don't know my wife, do you?" said Todd.

They walked off, leaving Ellie in front of the pool. *Calm*, she told herself. *Breathe.* Use the "breathing tool" they taught the kids at their school. Some kind of progressive mindfulness education that cost fifty Gs a year. "Mama, breathe," Giggy liked to say when she saw Ellie was losing it.

Ellie closed her eyes. She just wanted to get through this party and have it be a success. Wanted everyone to see how well she was doing, how big she had made it, how beautiful her family was, how much love and money she had won in life.

There was a small tap on her shoulder. "What?" she asked, thinking it was Todd, or Sterling. It was neither.

It was Nathaniel, who looked gray, and he was distinctly *not* carrying armfuls of new hydrangeas, or sunflowers, or whatever she had ordered him to procure. "I came straight from the office," he said.

"Okay."

"And, um . . ."

"What?"

"Mr. Kim called. He said he needs you to call him immediately."

"What? Why?"

"He wouldn't say."

Harry Kim was her Korean investor. She was selling half of her company to him to get an infusion of cash. That's how she pictured it—that his cash was going to be injected directly into her bloodstream. She needed it, that's for sure. Wild & West was deeply in debt, huge debt, and if she didn't get this deal finalized and funded, she would be late on her warehouse payments, late on her shipping orders, and late on her mortgages on her three houses. Not to mention late on four tuitions, and payroll . . .

Why did Harry need her to call him? What was going on? A cold feeling of dread snaked up from her heart to her throat.

She glared at Nathaniel. This was why they used to kill the messengers. No one liked bad news, and she had a feeling this was going to be awful.

"Another?" asked Victor, materializing at her elbow with another martini.

"Yes," she said gratefully. For once, she was glad he made the drinks too strong. She would need a lot more vodka before the night was through.

SIX

Some Kind of Something

October 19
Twenty-Four Years Ago
6:00 P.M.

Nordstrom's Brass Plum sold cheap shit to teenagers while their mothers shopped in the designer sections. It was by far the nicest store they'd ever been in, and there was a guy in a tuxedo, playing piano in the middle of it. The soothing tinkle of the keys even *sounded* more expensive than the cheap pop songs blasting from overhead speakers at the other shops. Maybe if they were more ambitious, they would have shopped in the fancier sections, scored bigger game, but Mish warned that they'd stand out too much. Better to keep to a place where people expected teenagers to be.

Leo riffled through the racks, humming along to the *Cats* theme on the piano, letting her touch linger on a particularly soft wool jacket, or a nubby leather one. She'd cleaned up in the bathroom beforehand, tied her hair back, pulled her shirt down, and tried to look like just another rich kid from the south side, thinking of Shona's offhand, casual style, like she wasn't even trying to look good but did so anyway. Mish was already in the dressing room, loaded up with loot.

Shoplifting wasn't their idea, at least not at first. They'd stolen it from a girl they'd noticed one day at Macy's. The girl didn't go to their high school, and she looked just like all the other teenage girls at the store, nondescript, a little sloppy. She was carrying a big slouchy handbag, and Leo would never have noticed anything amiss if the girl hadn't nonchalantly plucked one of the Mother's Day perfume-and-lotion gift boxes from the glass countertop right in front of them and placed it in her bag. Leo had elbowed Mish, and the two of them followed her around the store, watching keenly as the little thief methodically took another perfume bottle, a bracelet, a pair of earrings, and an eye-shadow kit.

On the second floor, the girl selected a large amount of clothing and soon disappeared inside a dressing room, only to reappear with a much smaller bundle, which she returned to the saleslady. The girl didn't look guilty or innocent, her face was blank, and she didn't notice the two of them practically stalking her. They looked around to check if anyone was following the girl. Did anyone see? Was security aware? But the girl waltzed out of the store with her big bag of pilfered goods, and nothing happened.

No alarm bells rang, no security guards ran out to apprehend anyone.

The girl had gotten away with it.

Leo and Mish turned to each other and grinned.

So now, when they went "shopping," this was what they meant. Shopping without paying. But they had to. Come on, they had no money, and it was so expensive to be a girl. They needed mascara, and lip gloss, and cute clothes and pretty underwear. Everyone else had all the right things, the right jeans and the right shoes and the right makeup. It wasn't fair.

So whatever they couldn't afford, they took. They couldn't afford a lot, so they took a lot.

The first time Leo tried, it didn't even count. She'd found a cashmere sweater without a price tag or even one of those security clips. She carefully put it around her waist, and walked out with it. A real cashmere sweater! For nothing! She couldn't believe it. The high was amazing. She couldn't wait to do it again.

Mish was even better at it. Mish was shameless. She took electronics, Nintendo game consoles, fancy headphones, and once even a portable telephone. Mish tended to wear baggy sweaters anyway, and stuffed her pants with lip liners and designer sunglasses and winter scarves. She was like a hibernating bear, fat with stolen goods.

Leo tended to be pickier about what she stole, although with shoplifting, timing played into opportunity, and even if she didn't really want those leather gloves, or an alarm clock, or a hand massager, she took them anyway, because no one was looking. Right now, she was shopping for her birthday outfit. No way in hell was she celebrating in worn jeans and a flannel shirt that had been washed way too many times. She had the black dress her mom had made in her bag, and she wanted cute cowboy boots and maybe a jacket to go with it.

She understood that if she got caught, it was over. She'd heard the rumors—that if you didn't carry ID, you could give them a fake name and they would let you go. But Mish had worked at

Sears one summer and told her that wasn't true; they just took you down to the station and booked you there. Then you had a record. Then if you ever committed another crime, they would see that it wasn't the first time, and once you had a rap sheet, it would be harder and harder for anyone—the police, the judges—to take pity on you. At least that's how Mish explained it. Leo should know this too, since her dad was still in jail, but Mish seemed to know more about the criminal justice system.

One of the tricks Leo had learned was to pretend to glance at the upper shelves of merchandise, when really she was looking for security cameras. She glanced up, and the nearest camera was several feet away, so she took a small handbag and stuffed it into her own larger one, and grabbed three leather jackets and five pairs of jeans and headed to the dressing room.

Mish was already walking out of it empty-handed, but with a bulging backpack. "What'd you get?"

Leo showed her. "I want to see which size fits," she said, as cover for taking three identical jackets, in case someone was watching.

"Cool."

There was no one in the dressing room; all the rooms were open and unlocked, with nary a salesperson in sight.

Once inside a room, Leo changed into her black dress, clipped the price tags off the jacket she wanted and tossed them into her bag, then slipped the jacket on. It fit perfectly. Real leather. Even if she saved all her money, she would never be able to afford anything like this. It was why they'd shopped at thrift stores until they started doing this instead.

Leo sucked in her breath, willing herself calm. She deserved this. She needed this. It was her birthday. She wasn't going to jail. Not today! Not ever!

She thought about heading over to the shoe department. New shoes might be too much to hope for. Those were harder to steal, as salespeople tended to hover while you tried them on. She ended up deciding not to risk it. She had her jacket; that was enough.

They walked out of the store. Nothing happened. They'd gotten away with it. Again. They smiled at each other as if they'd accomplished something.

"Hey, you weren't at the food court, so I thought I'd meet you here," said a tall, handsome boy at the entrance. So close that Leo bumped into him, her elbow brushing his chest. She looked up and smiled softly at him before she could hide it from Mish.

But Mish saw. And Mish narrowed her eyes.

Leo felt guilty, but a little part of her was defiant. Sure, he was with Mish now. But he'd wanted Leo first.

Because Leo was the one he'd seen, that afternoon, when Brooks had walked off the field, sweaty and cute from lacrosse practice, almost a year ago now. The weather was just starting to change, getting a little crisp in the air, and that afternoon, the light was hitting her hair just so, and she knew she looked good, dewy and young and pretty and innocent, in her jean skirt and a plain T-shirt and her tan. He'd said, "Hey." And she'd said, "Hey," back.

"You're a freshman, right?" he asked.

"Yeah, just started," she told him.

"How do you like it so far?"

She'd shrugged. "Same old crowd, new bullshit." She blushed; her mother had taught her, begged her, not to curse.

He'd grinned. "Not a fan of school, I take it."

They'd had a conversation that day, and over the next weeks, they had a couple more. He'd invited her to a party, and she told him she'd go and he promised to look for her.

But the night of the party, Leo had stayed home because her mom was strict and didn't like the sound of it, and Leo hadn't been brave enough to sneak out, to defy her. She'd stayed home like a good girl, but she'd told Mish about the party and Mish had gone alone.

The next morning, Mish had a row of hickeys around her neck, and she said Leo would never guess whom she'd made out with, and of course, without even guessing, Leo knew. She knew in the pit of her stomach. She knew who'd given Mish all those hickeys. Because they were supposed to be hers, supposed to be around *her* neck.

Because Brooks had chosen her first. He'd wanted Leo but ended up with Mish.

Mish got him. Because Mish always got what she wanted. And she'd always wanted Brooks.

The worst part, the part Leo couldn't deny, couldn't avoid, was that they actually liked each other. Maybe Brooks had been sort of interested in Leo once, but it was clear that he wasn't anymore. Maybe Mish was like a sex drug, maybe she had, like, a wonder vagina, a vagina that did magic tricks or something, because he was obsessed with Mish. He always had his hands all over her, and maybe it was just hormones or maybe that wonder vagina, but that boy was gone.

Brooks wrapped his long arms around his girlfriend and nuzzled her cheek while he spoke to Leo. "Hey, before I forget, happy birthday."

Leo looked down so they wouldn't be able to see her eyes. "Thanks."

"PICTURE!" Mish demanded, pulling away from his embrace. "Okay, you guys get together," she said, pushing Leo next to Brooks.

Leo grimaced a smile as Brooks gave a peace sign.

"Can you put that away?" she begged her friend.

Mish ignored her. "So, dude, what's the plan?" she asked Brooks. He shrugged. "I dunno."

Mish wheeled around. "You don't know? Wait, where is everyone? I thought you were going to bring the guys."

"Um, they're all going to Stacey's," he said sheepishly. "But Dave's here. He's at the food court."

"Dave?" asked Leo. There were a bunch of Daves at school. One of them was kind of cute.

"Yeah, David Griffin? You guys know him, right?"

Leo shook her head. The name didn't ring a bell.

"Brooks!" Mish swatted him playfully. "You were supposed to bring a bunch of guys! Not just Dave! Come on, it's her birthday!"

"I know, I know; *ow*, you don't have to hit me! I tried, babe!"

"Are you going to be this lame for my birthday next week?" Mish teased.

"Of course not," said Brooks, then realized he shouldn't have said that, considering Leo was right there. "I mean, this isn't lame . . . I mean . . ." he stammered.

One thing Leo couldn't stand more than anything was pity, and there was plenty going around right now. "You guys, it's fine," she said. "It's fine. Let's go meet Dave."

Mish rolled her eyes. "You sure?"

Leo widened hers. "It's so not a big deal. You know me!"

"Only if you're sure!" Mish insisted, and Leo could tell she was a little mad at Brooks for not coming through, that she did care, that she did want this to be a special night. Mish was her best friend.

"I'm sure." At least it wouldn't be just the three of them on her birthday. At least she wouldn't have to be the third wheel again.

Leo buried her feelings like she'd buried a silver bangle deep in the recesses of her handbag after pilfering it from the jewelry counter just a few hours ago, and smiled at her best friend and her best friend's boyfriend.

SEVEN

Twin Terrors

October 19
The Present
7:00 P.M.

Todd Stinson couldn't wait until this whole party, and this whole weekend, was over. It wasn't that he didn't want to celebrate his wife's achievements, her life, and entertain all her friends. He was proud of her and her success, and agreed it was important to take the time to mark the occasion; they had done the same for him five years ago, so it was all fine. And god knows they had attended enough over-the-top fortieth-birthday extravaganzas during the years. You'd think none of them had ever turned sixteen. There was that private island in Belize for Sanjay, yacht hopping in the Greek isles for one of her girlfriends, a bohemian weekend in Marfa for two artist pals; and Mean Celine had taken over the entire Amangiri hotel, with a dinner overlooking all of Canyon Point, including the famous Grand Staircase-Escalante. So he was used to excess. What he didn't like was being kept in the dark.

He sure hadn't liked it when Ellie bought this house on a

whim without discussing it with him first. It was August. She was out here with her girlfriends, the four of them sharing one room at the V downtown—one of those nice-enough motel renovations. It was an odd choice, since it wasn't even one of the newer or more luxurious properties in the area, but Ellie explained that even middle-aged women liked to feel like they were on a college trip, like they were young again at a big slumber party, and it amused everyone to pay so little for a room. Mean Celine had even smuggled in her Chihuahua because she refused to pay the pet fee since she wasn't staying the night. *Rich people.* Todd had rolled his eyes. The plan was to shop Rancho Mirage and maybe check out the Chanel and Gucci outlets if they had time. Ellie wasn't supposed to come home with a new *house*.

Sterling had been her coconspirator on this endeavor, pressing her to agree to a short escrow, no inspections, and fourteen-day close, and Todd would have held a grudge against him if he were that type. But Todd understood his wife's bulldozer mentality. Sterling knew nothing and no one would have stopped Ellie from having anything she wanted, and Todd should just be relieved Sterling was a legitimate broker and not a sleaze. When he'd sold his condo in LA, his neighbor had offered to list it, and Todd had agreed; the guy seemed nice enough. It was during the height of the bubble, when banks were handing out loans like lollipops, and the guy came back with an offer from a buyer that was way above market value. Except it was all a scheme—if Todd agreed to it, there was someone at the bank who would approve the buyer's loan, and all Todd had to do was kick back ten percent to his broker; oh, and leave the televisions. Todd was so insulted he threw the guy out and kept his TVs, even though they would end up buying a whole new set of flat-screens for the new layout in the new house. (And he ended up selling his condo for a fair price.)

He led Sterling to the master suite in the opposite wing. "We carpeted," he said, showing off the bedroom and the lush, creamy wall-to-wall. Todd liked stone in the public areas and Ellie had insisted on carpet for the private sections of the house. The stigma against carpet was an upper-middle-class tell. They were much richer than that; they could do whatever they wanted.

"Gold Calcutta marble," said Sterling admiringly, as Todd opened up the double doors to the master bath.

"We kept the Roman bath," said Todd, noting the step-down, built-into-the-ground Jacuzzi that was one of the most charming fifties aspects of the house.

The bathroom was all white and gold, with a crystal chandelier. They hadn't done much, just changed the ceramic tile to stone, but it had made a huge difference. Ellie looked even blonder in the bathroom.

"And you kept the vanity," Sterling said, admiring the built-in mirror and desk off the closet. "I'm so glad. Most people buy these legacy houses and just tear everything up. You kept all the bones."

"Ellie's a designer," said Todd.

"She told me you studied architecture," said Sterling. "How'd you get into TV?"

"I moved to LA," said Todd with a shrug. He'd studied architecture as an undergrad, then pivoted after finding out exactly how little first-year architects made. After business school, he had vague plans to go into real estate, or finance, but the network was hiring. Turned out he had a knack for it, and he fit the part—he was as handsome as the actors he hired and fired.

"Mr. Todd, Mr. Todd!" Citlali, their Palm Springs housekeeper, who had come with the house (as did the gardener and the pool man, bequeathed to them by the former owners), ran into the room, looking harried.

"The boys! They spilled . . ." she said worriedly.

"It's all right, Citlali," said Todd. "Sterling, if you'll excuse me. Twins are a handful."

Sterling raised his glass. "I'll give myself the rest of the tour. I know the house."

Todd followed Citlali down the length of the hallway. The house was laid out in a U shape, eight thousand square feet around the pool, with the golf course behind the hedges. Like most of the mid-century contemporary houses in Palm Springs, it was a one-story, sprawling. A few guests had begun to arrive, and he waved at them cheerfully but motioned to the housekeeper, making it clear he couldn't stop and chat right now. Citlali's slippers flip-flopped on the terrazzo as she jogged back to the game room.

Todd figured if the disaster was confined to the game room, nothing too terrible could have happened since it was furnished with comfortable sofas, billiard and foosball tables, and arcade games. What could those boys have spilled or broken?

The game room was empty and the twins were nowhere to be found.

"Hey, man," said the second DJ, a stoner from Cathedral City whom a friend of a friend had recommended.

"Hey," said Todd. "Is that a speaker?"

"Yeah." The DJ shook his head. One of the six-foot-tall speakers was lying sideways on the floor, broken, with bits of metal and plastic on the rug.

"They were fighting over the mic and pulled too hard," the DJ explained. "Your person tried to get them to stop."

Citlali kept shaking her head and muttering to herself.

Todd sighed. "How much?" A price was named. All in all, it wasn't too bad. "Add it to the bill," he said. "Will you still be able to play?"

"Nah, man."

Todd would have to remember to apologize to Ellie for yelling at her for booking two DJs, since it was fortunate they still had the other guy. The fancy DJ from the Las Vegas club was playing music in the main part of the house. Then again, it wasn't the fancy DJ's speaker that was busted. But it could have been, knowing the boys.

Todd brushed his hair back from his forehead. "Where are the twins?" he asked Citlali, who was sweeping the rug as the DJ began to pack up his equipment.

"They ran away."

Todd went to find them. They were probably outside on the golf course, taunting golfers. Another hobby of theirs, he thought with a grin. Those terrors. He couldn't stay mad. In truth, he wasn't even mad in the first place.

The twins were a hurricane; they left havoc in their wake. The family once went to dinner at a popular Mexican restaurant in Rancho Mirage, and Otis had climbed on the table to try to get a tortilla chip from the basket but fell on his butt, his sneaker landing in the salsa, which flew everywhere. He and Ellie had been so embarrassed, hurriedly gathering all the kids and getting out of there, but they also couldn't stop laughing when they got home.

He had four children. Sam was his eldest, his joy, his baby, but he had left her mother and he would never be able to make it up to her; she would forever feel the sting of that abandonment. Even if Sam liked Ellie, loved her even, she would always know that her father had chosen Ellie over his own family. Then there was Giggy, who loved him from the beginning, then hated him when she found out he wasn't her "bio-dad." That had cost a lot of therapy and he still resented the fact that Ellie hadn't let him adopt Giggy when they had the chance.

But the twins. Oh, the twins.

Elijah Samuel and Otis Benedict.

They were angels. Identical white-blond angels with their tanned little bodies. They ran rampant throughout every resort they'd ever stayed in. Ellie liked to keep their hair long; she never took them for haircuts. They looked like wild, feral, beautiful children. The boys could do no wrong. The girls liked to complain that Eli and Otis got away with everything, that their parents loved the boys more.

They weren't wrong. But they weren't quite right either. It

wasn't that they loved the boys more—it was just that they were easier to love. Was that a fair thing to say or think? Todd was pretty sure he loved all his children equally, even as they came to him under different circumstances.

The thing was, each girl was living with only one of her parents, a product of broken promises and broken homes. The girls knew that fairy tales sometimes didn't have happy endings. They knew and saw that their parents were flawed and sometimes made bad decisions. But to the twins—their parents had *always* been in love and *they* were the loves of their lives.

Besides, the two girls spoiled their brothers to death. The twins were everyone's favorites.

"Boys!" called Todd as he walked through a hole in the hedges in the backyard and continued on to the golf course.

Eli was chucking golf balls into the air while Otis was trying to get the golf cart to start. Thank god it was late in the day so there were no golfers around to complain. Not that anyone ever did. The boys lived in a bubble—every naughty prank they pulled only made them more endearing. Everyone at the golf club adored the twins, no surprise there.

Todd shook his finger at them. "Behave yourselves, okay? No more fighting. You broke the DJ's machine. Not good."

"Sorry, Daddy," said Eli, who was the sweeter one.

Otis looked petulant. "It was Eli's fault."

"It's both your faults," said Todd automatically. "You hear me?"

Otis pouted. "Yes, Daddy."

Todd looked down at them sternly. "What's today?"

"Mama's birthday party," whispered Eli.

"And what did we say you had to do today?" asked Todd.

"Be good," chorused the boys.

Todd ruffled both of their heads. They were like baby chicks, their hair as soft as feathers and as bright as the sun. "All right, let's go inside the house, and don't run away again; you guys can have dessert early."

Okay, so the girls were right, he did love them more. Shoot him.

EIGHT

Food Fights

October 19
Twenty-Four Years Ago
7:00 P.M.

Leo followed Mish and Brooks as they led the way to the food court. Mish and Brooks each had a hand in the other's back pocket, so they were cupping each other's butts as they walked. Why was that even allowed in public? Leo cringed to see it but she was jealous too, of course.

David Griffin was leaning against the wall near the hot dog and lemonade stand when they got there. Leo recognized him now. He was not the cute Dave. He was a little on the short side, with cropped dark hair and a wide grin. He was the guy who was forever walking down hallways and flipping up cheerleaders' skirts.

"Hey, hey," he said, when he saw them. "Birthday girl, huh?" he said, turning to Leo.

"Yeah," she said. "Thanks," she added, even though, technically, he hadn't wished her a happy birthday, just stated the fact. It would be something she would remember later, that he'd been a creep from the start.

"Let's get a picture!" said Mish, who appeared to be determined to record every awkward moment of this day.

Leo grimaced as Dave put his arm around her.

"Sweet sixteen. Tell me, how sweet is it?" he said, wagging his eyebrows as if he were funny or clever.

Leo glanced at Mish, who rolled her eyes. "Dave, don't be gross," said Mish. Leo extracted herself from his embrace. Mish put away her camera.

"You guys hungry?" asked Brooks hopefully.

"Not yet," said Mish, even though Leo could have used a little snack.

She spoke up then, and internally chastised herself for being so quiet. Leo did that sometimes, let Mish run everything. "Actually, I could eat something."

"Oh," said Mish. "Okay, what do you want?"

"Anything," said Leo. "Whatever." Her boldness went only so far; she was back to being agreeable.

Dave made it clear he found this indecision boring and turned to talk to Brooks about an upcoming lacrosse game, which he kept calling "lax" to be cool.

"Pretzels?" asked Brooks, who had been paying attention to the girls' conversation after all.

"Sure," said Leo, determined to be amiable even as she did the food math of pretzels = carbs = fat. The modeling scout had ordered her to lose weight, but she could start next week maybe.

They went and got pretzels from one of the concessions, and sat down at a table to eat. Dave didn't seem that interested in her, and the feeling was mutual. Brooks appeared a little tense, not relaxed like he usually was around them. Like he was trying to be more of a guy's guy because Dave was there. Usually he gossiped with them about everything that was happening in school.

Mish wasn't having it either. This birthday was turning out to be a bit of a dud. *I'm sorry*, she mouthed.

It's okay, Leo mouthed back. She took a bite of her pretzel because she was hungry, but it tasted leaden in her mouth.

"Brooks, can I talk to you?" asked Mish, pulling him away from the table.

"Sure, babe."

They left Dave and Leo alone at the table. Leo had no idea what to say to him, not that she didn't know how to talk to boys. She talked to Arnold a lot. Except she didn't really consider Arnold a boy, per se, he was just Arnold. Mostly, Arnold listened. Leo thought most people would choose David Griffin over Arnold Dylan any day. Dave had that clean-cut all-American look, while Arnold looked, well, dirty. Like a little filthy, like he lived on the streets, which he had to sometimes.

Dave continued to eat his pretzel in big, wolfy bites and ignored her. She took a little bite of hers. "Have you always played lacrosse?" she asked politely, to break the silence.

He shrugged. "I guess. I play soccer too. And baseball. But I had to choose a spring sport, so I chose lax."

"What position do you play?" asked Leo, who had no idea what kind of positions there were.

"Lead attack," he said smugly, although it meant nothing to Leo.

"Cool," she said.

"Damn straight it is," he said.

The conversation went like that: one-sided; he never asked her any questions about herself. Not even if she'd ever seen a lacrosse game, which she had. Mish dragged her to watch Brooks sometimes.

There were twenty players on the Arlington lacrosse team and any one of them would have been preferable to David Griffin. Noah Limerick, for instance, had a sweet smile, or Josh Pierce, who had a goofy sense of humor, or even Kurt Evans, Ryan Jones, or Patrick Ortega, who were all catalog-handsome.

Leo hoped Mish and Brooks would come back to the table soon. When they finally did, Leo tried not to look too relieved.

Dave got up. "Dude, I'm going to jam."

"Yeah?" asked Brooks.

"Yeah, I gotta meet everyone at Stacey's," he told them. "You'll be there, right?"

Brooks looked to Mish.

Mish shook her head.

"Okay, man, your loss," said Dave. He slapped Brooks's back and nodded to Mish. He didn't even say goodbye to Leo.

Mish took a deep breath. "You know what we need?" she said, her eyes sparkling.

"What?" asked Leo.

"Drinks. Come on. It's time we got this party started for real."

NINE

Cocktail Hour and the Billionaire Problem

October 19
The Present
7:00 P.M.

While Todd was handling some sort of mess in the game room, Ellie had her own problems. Her billionaires were starting to arrive, and billionaires always ruined it for everybody. Ellie wasn't sure she would have gone to all this trouble, flown so many people out, insisted on out-of-season flowers and fruit, hired the Parisian interior decorator, and booked two different DJs, if Blake, Celine, and Sanjay weren't coming tonight. If it was de rigueur to have at least *one* billionaire in one's social circle, Ellie of course had *three*. Billionaires were the new show ponies. Who *didn't* have a close personal friend who was a billionaire these days? In 1982, there were only twelve billionaires in the United States, but by 2012, there were exactly four hundred twenty-five superrich souls. They infected society like overfed beasts, brimming with the indifference and disdain that a billion dollars conferred on a person, living, as they were, in a shellacked billion-dollar bubble.

One of Ellie's LA girlfriends, Diana, a writer, had gone to high school with MacKenzie Bezos even. But Diana wasn't jealous that her old friend had ended up with a billionaire; instead, Diana was *incensed* that MacKenzie got better reviews for her first novel than she did, just because she was a Bezos. It was all Diana talked about when MacKenzie's book came out, how unfair it was that *The New York Times* had raved about it while they'd completely ignored her own book.

Ellie was amused but, unlike Diana, she was definitely jealous of the billions, especially since, with the divorce, MacKenzie would be the richest woman in the world. Numbers mattered to her. Ellie didn't know Jeff and MacKenzie or the mistress, but she knew people who knew them, which was enough.

Blake Burberry was the worst but the most famous, with a last name that was practically synonymous with Britain, a name that came with its own plaid pattern. In fact, Blake never signed his notes, since his personal stationery already carried the Burberry logo. Maybe he wasn't titled or royal (Blake spent his childhood playing tennis at Buckingham Palace with Prince William—okay, only twice, but an anecdote he let slip at every occasion), but his money wasn't brand spanking new and combustible like those Silicon Valley *paper* billionaires either. (What on earth was a paper billionaire? Was it like a straw man? Something not quite real?) Blake liked to think of himself as a contrarian, down-to-earth, frugal, and so in London he lived in Soho rather than Mayfair; in New York he hunkered down in Brooklyn Heights rather than the Upper East Side, drove a Mini rather than a Tesla, and was currently staying at the Ace Hotel rather than the Parker, which he deemed too extravagant. And yet Blake was also building a fifty-million-dollar Malibu house and flew his beloved Goldendoodle private for vet checkups back in New York. Blake was an ass.

They'd met in London, when she was still married to Archer. She could blame her ex-husband for the number of billionaires in her life, she supposed. Blake had been younger then, and cuter, and could get away with saying all those flippantly rude things in that posh accent of his. All she knew was she'd grown up dying to wear one of those iconic checkered scarves that she could never afford. When she met Blake, almost twenty years ago now, he'd been sweet even, but after coming into his trust fund and giving up his musical career due to an obvious-to-everyone-except-him lack of talent, he had hardened into a bored, listless dilettante. Bisexual and perennially single, because not even a billion dollars could make anyone put up with Blake (which was really saying something).

She had no idea why they were friends or if they even liked each other. But then, she could probably say that about half the people at the party. At least he'd dressed up for her, was wearing a slim Tom Ford navy suit and a crisp white shirt, tan and handsome. Ellie liked her friends to be decorative, to look good in a room. She approved. Apparently, so did he.

"Darling, you've finally impressed me," he smirked as he entered the house.

"Thanks, I think?" she said sharply. "What does that mean?"

"Oh, *Elle*," he said, "I'm just joking." Her never called her by her preferred name; she suspected he thought it was too gauche.

He disappeared into the party, zooming in on the friends they had in common, for he never had any interest in meeting anyone new since, as a billionaire, he figured he'd already met everyone worth knowing; everyone else wasn't worth his time. The party bus from the Parker had arrived a few minutes before, and by now the house was packed with out-of-town friends as well as a few locals they'd met through the museum. The London contingent seemed to be getting along with the New York people. The LA people hung together, cliquey as usual, but overall, there was a happy buzz over the sound of the piano and the cocktail shakers, which was the real music to her ears.

Of course, billionaires were the least of her problems. The moment she was alone, she snuck out the front door, pulled out her phone, and began texting Harry Kim to find out what was going on. She'd rung him the minute Nathaniel told her about the message, but he hadn't picked up, so she'd texted a barrage of questions right after. But so far, there was no answer, not even the dot-dot-dot that meant he was typing a reply. Nothing. This could not be good.

She could feel nervous perspiration forming on her brow and under her arms and she willed it away. The last thing she needed was to ruin her artfully made-up face and soak through the thin silk fabric of her dress.

With relief, she noticed a boxy Honda with an Uber sticker pulling up to the curb, which meant Sanjay was here.

Ellie had assumed that all the billionaires in her life would want to know one another, but while Sanjay was curious about Blake, Blake had absolutely no interest in Sanjay. Unlike Blake, who'd inherited his wealth, Sanjay had made his own money, had earned it in his lifetime. Sanjay Kumar was another of Archer's friends—although *friends* wasn't quite the word—more like Sanjay was one of the rich people in London whom Archer invited to his parties. Like Blake, Sanjay was a certified bachelor, but he preferred to date sexy MIT professors rather than Archer's host of jailbait models or Blake's pretty, young rent boys. Sanjay had helped Ellie out of a bad situation back when she and Archer were living in Dubai for a spell, and for that she was forever grateful; even after the divorce, they had remained friends, actually closer than ever. She liked to tell people she'd won the friends in the divorce; okay, correction, she liked to tell Todd, as a warning. But it seemed he already knew. (*"Your* friends.")

Sanjay was wearing his hedge fund uniform, a polo shirt and shorts, and he arrived at the party with his current girlfriend, who ran a tech company and boasted impressive Michelle Obama arms.

"What's wrong?" said Sanjay as a greeting.

"Is it that obvious?" She laughed weakly.

"Only because I know you," he said with a smile. "You remember Monica."

She did and kissed and hugged her graciously. "Bar's outside; try not to die in the heat."

"Go ahead," said Sanjay. "I'll join you in a minute."

"You didn't have to get rid of her," said Ellie when Monica disappeared inside the house. She sighed. She couldn't hide much from her old friend. "What's wrong with me? Nothing, everything."

"Is it Todd?" asked Sanjay. "You guys fighting again?"

"Yeah, but that's old news. When aren't we fighting? No, it's money. It's always money." It felt so much better to say it aloud. She grasped her phone and took a surreptitious look to see if Harry Kim had texted back. Nope.

Sanjay crossed his arms. "Money. Who cares about money?"

"Easy for you to say, Mr. Billionaire." She'd been teasing him this way for years, ever since she intuited how rich he really was. There was a fellow mom at Glenwood Prep, where the kids went to school, who made a habit of googling everyone's net worth and then kissing up to those who made the cut. Ellie never had to resort to that kind of web sleuthing. If someone was superrich in her circle, she knew about it instantly: It was in the air, whispered and talked about so much, the aura of a billion dollars like a heady perfume, that you knew everything about the billionaire before you even met them.

"I'll give you some money. How much do you need?" Sanjay offered.

"Are you serious?"

"Yeah, why not? Pay me back when you can."

"Sanjay, I couldn't. Thanks, but no." He'd offered before, and she always turned him down. Taking his money would change their friendship, and he was one of the few real friends she could count on.

"You've made your thirty million," said Sanjay. "What could be the problem?"

"Ha," she laughed faintly.

Thirty million. "After thirty million, it's all the same," Sanjay had told her once when they were having lunch in his building in New York, in the private restaurant in the lobby that was for residents only. Over at the next table was the CEO of Goldman Sachs, who was Sanjay's neighbor and Parcheesi playmate. "There's truly nothing out of your range after that."

"So after thirty million, there's nothing left to aspire to? That's as good as it gets?" she'd asked.

"Pretty much."

Sanjay spent as much as she did a year, they both lived at about three million dollars net, which meant he was frugal and she wasn't. But it did mean they took a lot of family vacations together, and met up at Art Basel Miami Beach in December, Aspen in January, and the Hamptons or Positano over the summer, if their schedules allowed. Sanjay was her only friend who ever called her on the phone instead of texting, and she suspected they were that close because he'd never been in love with her and vice versa. She was too stupid for him, she liked to joke (although it was true). But maybe they'd never been lovers because she'd done the same thing he did, white-knuckled her way, fighting and clawing to the top of the point-zero-zero-zero-one percent. They were allies, comrades. Sanjay had one child, a daughter from a previous girlfriend, his only heir, and it was Ellie's dearest wish that one of her twins would win Isadora Kumar's hand one day and make them a real family. Plus, all that lovely money couldn't hurt.

All this talk of money was making her stomach churn. If Harry Kim pulled out of the deal, she was fucked. She needed that deal like her life depended on it *because* her life depended on it.

"Seriously, Ellie Belly, what do you need?"

"From you, honey? Nothing," she said. "Seriously. I'm okay. Don't worry about me. It's nothing I can't fix." She couldn't tell Sanjay how badly in hock she was to the bank. It was too humiliating. How all this—the party, the house (all her houses), her entire life—was on borrowed time and money, and if that deal with Harry didn't come through, she wasn't even sure if she could pay the caterer tonight, let alone the two DJs.

She had to change the subject before she sweat through her dress and ruined it. "Forty years, can you believe I'm this old?" she asked.

"Um, no," he said. "Although I thought for sure you'd never admit to it. Models never do. I mean, I don't remember you ever turning thirty. Only twenty-five, five times." He shot her a cheeky grin.

"I was hoping to push it off for a *few* more years," she confessed.

"With that Botox you could've gotten away with it. By the way, I love your house," he said admiringly.

"Thanks, so does Blake. He said I 'finally' impressed him," she said wryly. She kind of liked that Blake had been so rude; it gave her a juicy anecdote to tell everyone at the party.

"Asshole."

"Douche."

"Why are you even friends with him?"

"I ask myself that question every time," said Ellie. "Maybe I'm just a sucker for nostalgia. He reminds me of being young in London."

"*I* remind you of being young in London."

"You're right. I guess I should get rid of him."

"You say that every time, and you never do. It's fine. I have a new little venture he might be interested in," said Sanjay, who was always working. "Anyway, this house! It's fantastic. It's so much better than mine."

"What are you talking about! I love your Hamptons house!" she cried. "This is nothing!"

Sanjay was forever lamenting the state of his beach house, which never seemed to live up to his expectations, and they talked about renovations and remodeling, the problem of architects and contractors, the headaches of permits and fees, the merits of Caesarstone versus veined marble. Rich-people chatter. To be rich in America meant to be in a state of constant renovation. Their conversation was interrupted by the arrival of Mean Celine, aka billionaire number three.

"Happy birthday, cupcake!"

"Mean Celine!" Ellie gushed as Sanjay made a graceful exit to let them catch up. "You made it!"

"We just touched down," said Mean Celine, who had a habit of flying her jet to events and then flying back home at the end of the evening, as she was allergic to "hotel sheets" and preferred the comfort of her own bed—by far the ultimate privilege.

Mean Celine's husband bought and sold airplanes and airplane parts to airlines all over the world, and thus Mean Celine was always telling her friends which airlines to avoid. "Oh god, never fly that shitty airline; they buy the oldest planes in our fleet!"

Mean Celine knew that everyone called her Mean Celine and she found it amusing, if a little too on the nose. She owned LA's two basketball teams and ran the boards of the philharmonic, the art museums, and the best private schools in the city, as well as every university that mattered in the area, including all the way to Stanford, which mattered the most. Outside of Hollywood, where she had little to no interest (Hollywood money was insignificant compared to hers), she was hands-down the most feared woman in all of Los Angeles: She wielded her money like a knife. She had taken Ellie under her wing years ago. Mean Celine's youngest daughter was Sam's best friend since seventh grade.

Or at least Alex used to be Sam's best friend.

Things were a tad frosty between the two of them lately, ever since Alex and Sam had started their freshman year at Stanford. The girls had had their ups and downs before, especially in ninth grade when they somehow ended up in warring cliques. But not like this. Sam complained Alex was "clingy" at college, while Alex told her mother that Sam was acting stuck-up. Privately, Ellie thought that it was because Sam had finally hit her stride and found her place among the supergeeks, while Alex, who didn't have the grades or the scores but whose last name graced the auditorium, was the one who was out of her element for once.

"Is that Sam? She came home for the party? How sweet. If I knew she'd be here, I would have made Alex come with," said Mean Celine, who seemed to have decided to pretend that the girls were still besties.

"I didn't know she was going to be here," said Ellie, who wasn't about to admit to any failure on Sam's part, especially not to Mean Celine.

Mean Celine popped a caviar-and-potato-chip confection into her mouth from a passing tray and shook her head. "How's that new boyfriend of hers?"

"Sam's? You mean she *finally* has a boyfriend?" she asked, shocked into blurting a truth. Sam had never dated anyone, ever. Which was why Ellie was wondering if she might be gender-fluid or something.

"Yeah, something like that, I think."

"She hasn't said anything to me."

"Well, you are her mother," said Mean Celine. "Last to know." Mean Celine looked around at the house and the party, and Ellie braced herself for criticism. This was the billionaire problem right here, the fear that you would never be good enough for those who could not only afford the best but could buy the entire world.

But Mean Celine was gracious. "You look gorgeous, not a day over twenty-five, doll. You and your good genes. And the house is perfection. This is the Gulf House, right? You know I grew up going to this house; my parents were friends with the Gulf family."

"Of course you did," said Ellie. That was another thing she noticed. All the rich people in her life knew one another. Sanjay was on the board of Mean Celine's husband's company, and Mean Celine knew Blake's mom socially. Sometimes, Ellie felt dizzy at the heights she'd scaled, that she was welcome, if not celebrated, in such company. These were her friends. People who knew when the market would tank before the market tanked.

People whose money pushed the world in a certain direction. People who knew which airlines to fly and which to avoid, even as they flew their own private planes around the world. Todd was forever asking about when they would get their own jet. Not yet, but hopefully soon, she'd told him. And even on borrowed money, they didn't have enough for a jet, only a jet share at the moment. It grated.

At least she wore real diamonds. "Celine, are those . . . ?" she asked, her fingertips brushing her friend's dangling rocks, as big as robin's eggs.

"Aren't they great? I got them at Claire's!" she hooted.

Mean Celine could buy all of Cartier and Harry Winston with the snap of her fingers, yet wore ten-dollar paste. She also carried a fake Chanel handbag. Since everyone assumed everything she owned was real, why should she spend the money? It was just a waste. Ellie shook her head. Rich people.

Sanjay returned with another round of drinks and escorted Mean Celine out to the pool, leaving Ellie in the hallway with her thoughts.

So many billionaires. So little time. If she were a billionaire, she'd have white tigers on jeweled collars and the hottest chicks from Crazy Girls dancing in cages above the pool, fireworks shooting out of their pasties. Sanjay's idea of a good time was a game of backgammon. Oh, he had his fancy wine collection and the annual white truffle auction in Hong Kong that he chaired for charity, where he and his fellow ten-figure friends bid on certain Italian pigs' ability to root out the tubers. But the man was just as happy with a McDonald's meal.

Blake's new hobby was his publishing empire; he liked to rescue newspapers and magazines for sport, run them into the ground, then toss them in the trash like, well, yesterday's news. Mean Celine *worked*, raising money for all those schools and endowments and scholarships, and bought fake diamond earrings at the mall.

Boring.

Ellie wouldn't do any of that. She would be such a *fun* billionaire.

Except of course, she was broke.

TEN

Mountain Dew and Vodka

October 19
Twenty-Four Years Ago
7:30 P.M.

The first order of business for any celebration, especially a sixteenth one, was the procurement of alcohol. Arlington kids sent their nannies or housekeepers to fetch the stuff. Old Filipino and Guatemalan ladies hobbling out of liquor stores with fifths of cheap bourbon, handles of vodka, gin, and tequila, along with cases of beer. Stacey was a shoo-in at Dartmouth next year, for hers was a legacy application; her dad was an alum. But right now, her parents were away, leaving her with a college-age babysitter who was only too happy to buy alcohol for a bunch of high school kids, especially since she charged them a fee for the service.

Unfortunately, Leo and Mish weren't rich and didn't have nannies to send to the corner store, and Brooks didn't have a fake ID. Still, all they needed was maybe a six-pack of beer or a few wine coolers, or maybe a bottle of vodka? Leo had no idea. She never drank, never touched the stuff. She was a little afraid of it, to be honest. But she wanted some now. It seemed appropriate, and maybe even sad if there wasn't any. But nothing about her birthday was turning out the way she had hoped. She had depended on Mish to bring the fun, and Mish had depended on Brooks, but Brooks, it appeared, was far from dependable.

It wasn't even much of a party, just the three of them as usual now that Dave had ditched them. Maybe he didn't think she was pretty enough. Not that she cared, but it was insulting how quickly he'd disappeared. Maybe she should just go home. She still had the bus transfer in her pocket. Maybe her mom would get off work early. Maybe they could still get that Carvel cake after all.

"So, um . . ." she started to say, before Mish jumped at her again, eyes blazing.

"HELL NO!" screamed Mish, pointing her finger right at her face.

"Huh?" Leo said, taken aback.

"Babe?" Brooks crunched his forehead adorably.

Mish kept her finger pointed at Leo. "I know what you're going to say! You're going to say you're tired and you're going home and you guys should just leave me alone; well, fuck that! It's your birthday! We! Are! Celebrating!"

Leo laughed and took a step back. "Okay, okay!"

"You've got that awesome jacket, and we're going to party!" said Mish. "Right, Brooksy?"

"Yeah, of course," Brooks said, amused, and squeezing his girlfriend tight. "Whatever you guys want."

"You were supposed to bring some guys," accused Mish. "You failed in this endeavor. Even Dave left."

"I know, I know; sheesh, I'm sorry."

Mish put her hands on her hips. "And we can't just stay at the mall."

"We can't?" asked Leo.

She shook her head. "And we're not going to Stacey's."

"We're not?" asked Brooks.

"Why not?" asked Leo.

"Because we're not fucking celebrating your birthday at someone else's goddamned birthday party, that's why!" insisted Mish. "I mean, come on!"

"Okay," said Leo. She hadn't realized until then that it was Stacey's birthday too.

"Okay," said Brooks.

"Okay!" said Mish, mollified.

Brooks offered to drive to his house to try and get into his parents' liquor cabinet, which wasn't even locked. But Mish shook her head at that proposition. Leo wasn't sure if Mish didn't want to get caught by Brooks's parents, or if she didn't want Leo in his house again, but in the end, they ended up in the 7-Eleven back in Cully, in their neighborhood. There was a liquor store next door, where Mish procured a bottle of Gordon's, as well as a case of beer.

"I told them it was for my dad," she explained, walking out with the bulky brown paper bag. "They know him," she said curtly, in a tone that meant don't ask her any more questions.

Next they bought a liter of Mountain Dew and plastic cups and the three of them headed to the alley behind the store. It was

Mish's idea. It's what kids from their part of town did. Leo was a bit embarrassed, but at least they had alcohol.

Mish poured a ton of vodka into each of their cups and sloshed Mountain Dew on top of it. "Happy birthday!" she said.

"Happy birthday to me!" said Leo, holding her drink high. She took a big gulp and coughed. The liquor burned in her throat. People drank this? Willingly?

"Easy there," said Brooks with a toothsome smile, like some guy in a commercial. Did he have to be so cute?

Mish snort-laughed. "Drink up. Let's get *wasted*," she said, pouring even more vodka into Leo's cup.

Leo drank.

They were sitting on the curb, on their third round of drinks, now with a bag of Cheetos between them, when Mish declared she was bored and they could do better than sitting on a sidewalk, getting drunk. "What else is there to do in freaking Portland," said Brooks, a little annoyed. "Just woods, forests, woods and forest. Too many fucking parks."

"Woods Forest," snorted Leo. "That's where we live."

"We could go to the Ritz?" suggested Leo, meaning a popular coffee shop downtown.

Mish made a face. "Coffee? We want to get wasted, not sober."

"Come on, that's a fun idea," said Brooks.

"If she was turning forty maybe!" said Mish. She gulped down the last of her vodka. "No, let's go to Sparkle."

"We don't have IDs," Leo said. "How'll we get in?"

Mish rolled her eyes and peeled off her shirt without warning, so that she stood there, on the sidewalk, in her black bra. "We're hot. That's all we need to be. No one will card us, I promise! Come on!"

Brooks just grinned, enjoying the view.

"Fine, but I'm keeping my dress on," said Leo.

"Prude," said Mish, sticking her tongue out.

Sparkle was the biggest nightclub in the city that was also a live music club where all the coolest, best bands played if they were in town. If no one was headlining, the club had multilevels of DJs, one on every floor. It was Leo and Mish's dream to go there, but they'd never been brave enough before.

"Come on!" said Mish, pulling Leo up from the sidewalk.

"Coming," said Leo, wobbling. She'd never been drunk before, so she wasn't quite sure what was going on, but she knew she was warm, and slightly goofy, and taking off her dress suddenly wasn't such an outlandish idea. Everything was spinning and she felt extraordinarily brave and a little out of control, just like that afternoon when she lost her virginity all of a sudden.

Tonight, it felt like anything could happen. This was exactly what she wanted. Her birthday was shaping up to be fun after all. She just had to make her way to the back of Brooks's car. She could do that, she thought, even as she tripped a little on the sidewalk.

Deep breath.

One step at a time.

ELEVEN

No Such Thing as Bullying in Private Schools

October 19
The Present
7:30 P.M.

While his wife was busy entertaining the ten-figure set, Todd had somehow fallen into the managing-the-children part of the event. It was a position he wasn't unfamiliar with. Ellie liked to remark that he wasn't "babysitting" if he was with *his own children*. He had been unemployed for a while now and though he had spent the first several months furiously lunching with every colleague and connection, he hadn't followed up with any leads or offers and they had frittered away slowly. At the time, it didn't feel like he was the one consciously choosing not to do anything, just seemed that none of the projects or production companies willing to take him on felt "right" somehow. Did it *really* matter that he hadn't worked in two years? Ellie made more than enough money.

So even if he pretended to have been roped into chauffeuring drop-offs and pickups, he actually enjoyed seeing the kids on a regular basis since he did the morning school-run every day and picked up on Fridays, while Miranda handled the rest. Todd had missed so much of Sam's childhood that he was glad for the chance to do it over again with Giggy and the boys. There was always ice cream or Pinkberry after Friday pickup, which kind of added to the weight gain, but Todd found he couldn't deprive them when they asked, then begged, then threw a tantrum for it. It was easier just to give in from the start.

He was in the middle of a conversation with one of Ellie's old friends from London when he heard a loud wail coming from the side yard playground where they'd corralled the kids. Ellie had insisted on being able to have little kids running around her party—a strange tic of hers, but one that was endearing. Red wine or colored drinks were forbidden, but kids were always welcome at any of her events. Todd went to check it out immediately. He knew that wail.

When he walked into the playground, Giggy was sitting on the grass, crying her eyes out, while several girls from her school were huddled in the corner, whispering and watching. Only one of them was kneeling on the grass next to her, an arm on Giggy's shoulder.

"What happened?" he asked, his temper flaring instantly. He hated seeing any of his kids in pain. "Why is she crying?" he demanded.

Most of the girls who were huddled together shrugged and looked away. One of them boldly looked him in the eye and said, "We have no idea; she just started crying for no reason."

Little liar. He knew this kid. Her father was one of the top agents in the business. She was just as pugnacious as he was. Todd looked around hurriedly. Where was the playdate coordinator they'd hired to keep an eye on the kids? To make sure nothing like this happened?

A young Latina rounded the corner, carrying juice packs and string cheese. She had been Giggy's first-grade teacher and now taught the boys. If Todd thought it was odd that Ellie hired her to babysit the kids at her party, he tried not to think about it too hard. How much did elementary schoolteachers make? Miss Kayleigh probably needed it, right? They were doing her a favor?

"Oh, Todd! I'm so sorry. I went to get the girls some snacks. What happened?" she asked.

"They won't say," he told her. He knelt down so he was next to Giggy. "Can you tell us what happened? Were they bullying you?"

Giggy shook her head.

"See, she's fine," said Miss Kayleigh. "You're fine, right, Giggy? Sometimes the kids just get a little rough, that's all." That was the school policy: They stopped using the word *bullying* to describe aggressive behavior because there was no bullying in private schools. Especially not at the tuition they were paying.

Todd tried not to look too incredulous. "She's obviously not fine."

The little girl next to Giggy gave her a hug. "You're okay, Giggy."

"Thank you, Zoe," he told the little girl. He knew all of Giggy's friends and Zoe was particularly sweet.

He pulled Giggy up from the grass. "Come on," he said, even as she kept sniffing and wiping her nose with her sleeve.

———

They went to Giggy's room, which was also decorated in shades of white and gold with splashes of pink and green. She sat on one of the princess beds. There were two, and Sam had placed her suitcase on top of the other one, except Sam was nowhere to be seen. She was probably in the bathroom since the door was closed. The girls were supposed to share a room even though the other princess bed was really for Giggy's friends when they came for sleepovers.

"Gig, you're going to have to tell me what happened," he said.

"Nothing happened," she said sullenly.

"So you were just sitting there crying for no reason?"

"Correct," she said, with just a trace of an English accent since she had spent the weekend with her father, who was in town for the party.

Todd sighed. For a while he just sat next to her, rubbing her back. He'd learned not to push. At last, when she'd stopped sniffing, he brought it up again. "Can you tell me why you're upset?" he asked gently.

"They were teasing me," she whispered, kicking her feet against the duvet cover.

"What about?" he asked, even though he had an idea. There had been many emails from the school in the past few months. Ellie was supposed to be on top of it (Giggy being her biological child) but of course had been too distracted with running her company. Todd was the one who had gone to meet with the teacher.

"They said I was stupid," said Giggy.

"You're not stupid, you know that, right?" he said firmly.

She hung her head. "Maybe I am."

"No, you're not."

"I'm not smart like Sam," she said, her blue eyes blazing. She worshipped her older sister; all three of the little ones did. Sam was their hero and idol.

"You're smart in your own way, Giggy," said Todd.

"What way is that?" said Giggy sullenly.

Todd thought about it. He wasn't lying to her. He did think Giggy was smart, just not academic. "You're smart like your mom is smart."

"Really?"

"Yeah." He put an arm around his daughter. He remembered how she'd smelled as a baby, like milk and powder. Her skin was so white it was translucent. "Look at me, I did well in school, but I don't work anymore. Your mom never even went to college, and she can wipe the floor with everyone I went to Harvard with."

Giggy giggled.

"It's true," he said with a smile.

Stepdad had not been in Todd's vocabulary. His parents were strict midwestern Catholics; divorce was anathema, and blended families were regarded with pity. Of course he hadn't planned on getting married four—was it truly four?—times. It was amazing he had only four children really. His parents both came from large families, and one of Todd's uncles had ten children. Ten! Was it the nineteenth century or something? Who had ten children? Todd had no idea how much he disdained his upbringing until he left it—divorced his first, second, and third wives and left his only child and married a woman who already had a baby.

This baby.

He wanted Ellie so much he didn't care what she came with, didn't even really think about what it meant to marry a "single mom." But a baby wasn't luggage. Giggy was a person and, for the first four years of her life, called him Daddy. The problem arose when Archer came back into her life and Giggy discovered she and Todd weren't related to each other at all. She'd pulled away, confused as to how she could have two dads. He'd been hurt when Giggy started calling Archer "Papa."

Todd was her father. He was the one who found the private reading tutor. He was the one who made sure she had therapy. She wasn't a special-needs kid but she had special needs. She was so much harder to deal with than Sam, who was meek and quiet, and the boys, who were naturally lovable.

The problem was that Giggy called him out on his shit. She made arch comments about his penchant for video games, and loudly wondered why he was home all the time. She was ten years old and already as tough as her mother. She looked the most like Ellie too, with her fair coloring and delicate features.

Giggy leaned on his shoulder.

"Want to get ice cream? I told the boys they could get dessert early. Do you want some too? We could go to the kitchen and see what gelato flavors the chef brought."

She nodded.

Todd gave her shoulder a squeeze. Of all the things he had learned from being a more hands-on dad, it was that ice cream cured every ill. He thought of the party that was going on outside, and how peaceful it was in here.

"Maybe I'll have one too," he said.

TWELVE

Friends in High Places

October 19
Twenty-Four Years Ago
8:00 P.M.

Downtown Portland. Was there anything more depressing? Leo thought not. It was barely a city, just a couple of blocks of storefronts and warehouses, a couple of boarded-up stores, sleepy diners, seedy bars. There was supposed to be a transit rail system one day, and Pioneer Courthouse Square had opened just a few years prior, a slick new central park in the middle of the city. There was talk of revitalizing the waterfront, but so far, it was just talk. One day, she'd get out of this place, one day, she vowed, this city wouldn't be enough for her. She wouldn't rest until she was familiar with the streets of Paris and New York, when jetting off to London was as routine as taking the bus to the mall. One day. But for now, this was all she had. It was too early to get into Sparkle; the club didn't even open until nine, and the "good" DJ didn't start his set until after midnight.

"Pass me the nice drink," ordered Mish, one hand on the steering wheel while the other reached back to grab the red cup from

Leo's hand. Mish was driving because Brooks was way too plastered. He'd gotten in the car and hit reverse, almost knocking into a few trash cans. Mish had insisted she wasn't drunk at all and that she could drive.

So Leo had spent the ride passing the "nice drink" to Mish, praying to god that they wouldn't get in an accident. Please, Lord, don't let me die on my sixteenth birthday.

Brooks had passed out asleep in the passenger seat. "Lightweight," said Mish, trying to prod him awake after she found parking a few blocks from the club.

"Come on," said Mish, getting out of the car.

"Where are we going?"

"Anywhere!"

Leo scrambled out of the back seat. "We're just going to leave him here?"

"He'll be fine!" Mish yelled, slamming the door.

Mish led the way, through the dark city streets, passing convenience stores and diners, laundromats, tattoo parlors, and liquor stores. At least she had put her shirt back on. They were getting a little close to Burnside Bridge, which was always a little more sketchy, with more homeless people around. Leo was starting to worry.

"Do you know where you're going?" asked Leo, trying to keep up.

"No, do you?"

"Mish, what are we doing?"

"Killing time, looking for trouble, looking to score," she said, a crazed look in her eye.

"Score?" Leo scoffed. "Score what?"

"Drugs, silly!"

Leo made a face. She didn't do drugs and neither did Mish. Mish was just exaggerating again, trying to appear cooler than she was.

"It's your birthday!" screamed Mish.

"It's *been* my birthday all day. Come on. Let's just go back, just drive me home," said Leo.

"No."

Leo lunged for the keys in Mish's hands, but Mish was too fast for her. "Gonna have to catch me!"

"Come on, Mish, it isn't funny."

But Mish was laughing and held up the keys. "Want these?" she taunted.

Leo lunged again and missed. She felt like slapping the shit out of her friend. She was tired, drunk for the first time, and wanted to go home. But Mish wasn't done, and she was looking for trouble.

Thankfully, they found Arnold first.

Arnold Dylan was skinny-scrawny, with long bangs that fell into his eyes, and surprisingly tall, which no one ever noticed because he slouched so much. He'd dropped out of high school a few years ago but wasn't much older than them. The girls liked to say he was dirty-cute, filthy-sexy, like obviously a loser. But there was something about him nonetheless. Leo thought it was the eyes; Arnold had nice eyes and a sweet smile. He was rumored to deal, especially since he spent most of his time standing around corners all day.

"Arnold," Mish called. "Hey, hey, Arnold! You have something for us?"

Arnold shuffled over, his baseball cap pulled low. "What do you need?" he asked with a shy grin.

"Anything. What have you got?" Mish asked, crossing her arms against her chest with a serious look on her face.

"Anything?" he raised an eyebrow.

"Anything for free!" Mish said, laughing. "Come on, we're saving to get into Sparkle."

Arnold sighed. "Fine. But you owe me."

"We owe you!" said Mish.

"I'm going to collect," Arnold joked.

"Yeah, yeah," said Mish.

Arnold was always saying he was going to collect on the favors he did for them—giving them cigarettes, or buying them beer, or lending them a CD or a cassette tape. But he never did. He was the closest thing they had to a friend in their neighborhood. Mish was mean to him a lot, always telling him to get lost when the cigarettes were smoked and the beer ran out, or that if he wanted his copy back of the Smiths' *Meat Is Murder*, he had to buy another one. Leo felt bad about it sometimes, the way they treated him. Arnold didn't seem to mind, though.

"Wait here," said Arnold.

"Where are you going?"

"Get my stash," said Arnold. "One sec."

They watched as Arnold disappeared around the corner.

"Is he coming back?" asked Leo.

"Of course he is," said Mish confidently. "It's Arnold."

THIRTEEN

Whores d'Oeuvres

October 19
The Present
8:30 P.M.

D*id that asshole actually bring a hooker to her birthday party?*
Already on edge because Harry Kim had yet to text or call back and the stark reality of their financial situation was finally hitting her, Ellie found a new place to vent her rage. As she made the rounds, flitting between guests and introducing old friends to new, conferring with the party planner on when to start dinner service (hold it just another hour, she'd decided), she couldn't help but keep staring at a certain conspicuous couple. Melvin Ames was a short, bald, mega-successful producer of television shows of dubious entertainment value, a friend of a friend, a quasi-boldfaced name, and a classic LA douchebag whom Ellie had invited because they had bumped into him at the golf club that morning. "I'm having a birthday party tonight!" she'd chirped. "Stop by!" So there he was, in all his lecherous, dwarfish glory. And by his side was a very, very expensive piece of arm candy.

"Is that a fucking hooker?" she hissed, grabbing her husband by the elbow and steering him to look in their direction.

"What? Who? Huh?" said Todd. He squinted at the couple.

Was it her imagination or did Todd have chocolate on his upper lip? She wiped it off with her hand and he wrenched away from her touch, annoyed. "What are you doing?"

"You had a smudge," she said. "But back to Melvin's date, she's a pro, right?"

You'd have to be particularly eagle-eyed to even notice, for the girl was no ordinary call girl. This one was five-ten, Asian, gorgeous, and dressed in tight jeans, thigh-high boots, a Chanel purse slung on her shoulder (real, unlike Mean Celine's), and a gold Hermes belt wrapped around her twenty-four-inch waist. Why anyone would think she was a hooker rather than a model or an actress, only Ellie could explain. It was the whole package, from the too-tight clothes, too-shiny mane of black hair, and too much makeup, but it was the Hermes belt that really sealed the deal. *H* for *hooker*. No self-respecting actress or model ever splurged on designer clothing; they hoarded their money and wore samples from showrooms or cheap castoffs from set.

But hookers? Hookers spent, baby; they wore brand-name logos like merit badges. Blow-job Balenciaga. Anal Armani. Louis Vui-threesome.

"Maybe he's her sugar daddy," said Todd, shrugging.

"Which still makes her a whore," said Ellie, furious. "I want them out of here."

Todd sighed. "You invited them."

"Great! I can kick them out."

"Ellie."

"A *hooker*, Todd. The children are here. Sam is here. Have you spoken to her yet, by the way?"

"No, not yet, but I will. I'll find out what's going on. I was dealing with the boys and Giggy. The boys broke a speaker and the girls are bullying Giggy again."

Ellie wasn't listening. She was staring daggers at the Hollywood producer and his pricey date, willing for them to disappear. What would *Vanity Fair* think? What would her billionaires think? She hoped no one else would notice, even as she caught the other LA moms glancing over there and casting wary looks the girl's way. Maybe she was being too judgmental. She knew how hard it was, how rough it was to come from nothing.

But there was a hard line between modeling and dating rich guys and, well, *hooking*. Besides, the only rich guy she'd ever dated was Archer de Florent, and he *married* her. There was a huge difference. Ellie had used her looks to claw her way up the social ladder, to secure her business, to build her fortune, but she had never, ever, ever *sold her body* for any price. She would joke that she sold it only to the highest bidder, but that's all it was, *a joke*, and even if she was from the trailer park, she was still horrified and repulsed by the very idea of letting anyone touch you just for cash. She'd made many mistakes in her life, and had been young and stupid once, and she hated seeing the same desperation in other girls. It was too close a reminder of her own past.

Besides, she'd loved Archer after all, and therein lay the difference. Whoever this backdoor Betty was, she was definitely with Melvin for the cold, hard cash.

"Never mind her, who's that guy over there by the bar?" said Todd. "I don't think I know who he is. I've never seen him before."

Ellie froze. Was it *him*? She couldn't breathe for a moment. But when she looked over to where Todd was motioning, she saw that it wasn't. There was only a stranger, an older man, slightly out of place, eyes darting furtively around the party.

"No idea," she said. "Maybe someone's date?"

"He hasn't said hello to anyone," said Todd. "Maybe he crashed?"

"Out here? In Palm Springs?" Ellie scoffed. This was a far cry from the velvet-rope affairs of Hollywood shindigs or New York nightclubs. Their house was in a cul-de-sac, and no one knew about the party except people who had been invited. This wasn't an event that appeared on publicists' radars or in media press releases. It was private. Whereas during her youth in Manhattan, it had been almost blood sport to crash exclusive parties, and the most famous crashers even had nicknames like Shaggy and the Sultan, none of that existed in the desert. The strange man had to be someone's guest, a friend of a friend.

"Maybe he can leave and take the hooker with him," said Todd, who was uncharacteristically disturbed.

"I'm sure he's fine," said Ellie. "Don't make a scene."

Todd grunted and left to his mission.

Ellie sighed. Hookers and billionaires. Happy fortieth. She had everything she ever wanted, and then some. Or did she? She wanted to tell Sanjay he was wrong, thirty million wasn't enough; look at Johnny Depp, who was bankrupt too. Thirty million wasn't even close to cutting it. She was a huge, yawning pit of desire.

"You have a void in you," her therapist had said once.

"Oh, I know I do," she'd said, laughing. "I have a void in me that I fill with jewels and houses and husbands!"

Then she fired her therapist for telling her something so obvious. Of course she had a void in her, and no matter how much she had, she never felt satisfied, never fulfilled, always hungry. *More.* Archer hadn't been enough. And Todd—well—to be fully honest, Todd wasn't even her second husband. He was her third.

But she didn't count the first one. She'd erased him from her past and scrubbed every bit of him from her memories. She'd been so young! Too young to get married, for sure, which was why it had been easy enough to get it annulled after a few months. There was only Archer, then Todd. Who needed to know about the first guy? He wasn't important. The past was past. The past was history and so was her first husband.

But as a famous writer once said, the past isn't dead, it's not even past, which the presence of Todd's ex-wife at the party made abundantly clear. "Montserrat!" Ellie said, trying to sound sincere, as her husband's toxic ex-wife made her way to her.

"Ellie," she purred. "Happy birthday! Forty. Wow. I wonder what I'll do when I get to be that age! You're so brave!" Only Montserrat would equate courage with growing older.

Montserrat never failed to remind Ellie that she was all of five years younger. When Ellie had first married Todd, when they were still cuddly newlyweds, Montserrat would screech "HOW DO YOU LIKE FUCKING THAT OLD CUNT!" on his voice mails. But now the new and improved and *medicated* Montserrat would be horrified at her former actions. It had been years since she'd tried to run over Ellie with her car or knocked her down and pulled her hair during one of their violent, custody-battle drop-offs and pickups. Now Montserrat was the queen of the subtle knife, the underhanded diss, the undermining, left-handed compliment. In a way, Ellie missed the days when they'd resorted to punching and clawing at each other; at least back then they had been honest about their feelings.

Now they had to air-kiss and make nice.

Annoyingly, the bitch looked good. No wonder Todd had married her. She was a vixen, all bodacious curves in the right places with a flat tummy and tiny bubble butt, sex on a stick. She had almond-shaped dark brown eyes, skin the color of an iced latte, as beautiful as her daughter. Ellie felt a pang. No matter what, this was Sam's mother.

"How are you, how are the children? How's Giggy?" Montserrat asked, making a sad face. Montserrat never failed to rub it in that her child was a genius and Ellie's was a dum-dum.

"Imogen's great. The twins are great, everyone's great," said Ellie brusquely.

"Samantha said Giggy's moved on to another new tutor," Montserrat said smugly.

Ellie didn't take the bait, refused to play that game. She loved both her daughters, even the one who'd come out of this one. "When did you talk to Sam?"

"Oh," said Montserrat. "Isn't she here?"

"You know she's here?"

"Of course. She came to my house first. But I told her I was renovating and she should stay here." Montserrat had a cottage in La Quinta, which she bought years ago after the divorce came through. Ellie's victory lap when she bought Gulf House was that much sweeter, knowing that her husband's ex was stewing in a dinky little nine-hundred-square-foot bungalow while she had this grand, historic estate.

"Why is Sam home?" she asked.

"She didn't tell you?" asked Montserrat, feigning surprise.

"No."

Montserrat grimaced, and Ellie could tell she was actually upset this time. "I think she should be the one to tell you."

FOURTEEN

Poppers in the Alley

October 19
Twenty-Four Years Ago
8:30 P.M.

Arnold was gone for a while. Leo rocked back and forth on her heels. She was still a bit drunk from the vodka and Mountain Dew. "He's not coming back," she said.

"He totally is."

"How can you be so sure?"

"Because Arnold likes you," said Mish.

"What?"

"He told me."

"Oh," said Leo.

"I know he's like so old," said Mish. "And it's Arnold!" Mish made a face.

"He's like nineteen," said Leo. "That's only three years."

"Do you like him?"

Leo blushed. She hadn't really thought about it, but Arnold was cute in his own way. "I don't know, maybe, why?"

Mish huffed, then changed the subject. "I wish Dani were here, she was fun," she said, meaning Arnold's older sister.

"Yeah," said Leo, wondering why Mish would care whether she liked Arnold or not.

Dani Dylan was kind of a legend in the trailer park. She was loud, brash, and had a real mouth on her. The kind of girl Leo's mom told Leo to stay away from. Dani liked to say she was an accidental hooker, not a *hooker* hooker.

"I just met this guy at the club," she told them once, sucking on her cigarette. "And I slept with him in his hotel. The next day he leaves me like two one-hundred-dollar bills. He thought I was a prostitute!"

"Oh my god!" screeched Mish while Leo's ears went red.

That was last year. Mish told Leo her mom said she saw Dani the other day, getting out of a red Camaro. "Supposedly she's dating the manager of the Chili's where she works," said Mish. "A real sugar daddy."

"Gross," said Leo. "Isn't he like thirty?"

"Older, I think," said Mish.

Arnold finally returned. He looked left and right and took a seat on the sidewalk with them.

"Hey, how's Dani?" asked Leo. "We never see her anymore."

"She's all right." He shrugged.

Mish crossed her arms over her chest. "Heard she has a new boyfriend."

"I guess you could call him that."

"You don't like him?" asked Leo.

He shrugged. "Not really. But what's she going to do? Stay here. I mean, you know what I mean."

"Yeah." She did know.

"At least he doesn't beat her like the other one," said Mish.

Leo nodded. During the accidental-hooker phase, Dani had sort of slipped into real-hooker hooker territory. One of her boyfriends was also her pimp and beat her so badly she had to go to the hospital. Arnold never talked about it.

Leo thought that maybe Arnold looked out for them because they reminded him of his sister. Or maybe he was just nice. Sometimes he was the only person she could talk to who wouldn't judge.

"So what do you have for us?" asked Mish.

"Come see," said Arnold, pulling out a plastic bag from his jacket.

What Arnold had was poppers. "Have you done these before?" asked Leo as Mish stuck the tiny amber bottle up her nose.

"Yeah," said Mish, shrugging as if it were no big deal. "With Arnold." She and Arnold exchanged a look. Arnold frowned, as though embarrassed for some reason.

"These aren't like addictive," he explained. "I didn't give her crack. I would never."

"Arnold, do you even deal crack?"

He didn't answer, just looked uncomfortable.

Mish sucked in a breath and handed it to Leo.

Leo stuck it under her right nostril. "Now inhale!" said Mish.

She did. It burned, it felt as if it were frying her brains, like it went right up her nose and into her mind. It was dizzying. "Oh my god!"

"Right?" said Mish gleefully.

Leo started laughing hysterically.

"Take another hit," said Mish.

She did. And another. And another. Arnold joined them, snorting and laughing the loudest.

The three of them passed the bottle among them, laughing hysterically. The high lasted only a few seconds, but it was intense. Leo had no idea what was so funny, only that whatever was in the little bottle was like inhaling a lot of fun.

"Wait! Don't finish it; we'll need more for the club, when we get out to the dance floor," said Mish, taking the bottle back.

They smoked instead, Arnold once again providing for them. He shook out a couple of Camel cigarettes from his pack and they each took one. Leo's head was pounding from the alcohol and the poppers, so it felt good to slow down a little, smoke a little nicotine, which took some of the edge off. Arnold bought them beers from a deli and once more, they sat on a curb, drinking.

Mish took out the Polaroid once more and held it up. "Say cheese, you two," she said.

Leo and Arnold looked up from their beers. "Cheese!" they said, as the flash went off and the camera made a whirring noise and spat out another photograph.

"So, Sparkle, huh? Anyone playing tonight?" he asked.

"No idea," said Mish, sucking on her cigarette and blowing

smoke rings. Mish didn't seem too high or too out of it. She'd drunk the vodka like a pro, and while she laughed at the poppers, she seemed to be in control. But that was Mish—high tolerance, high maintenance, always cool.

In contrast, Leo felt as if she were out in a sea, a great big sea of illicit fun that she'd never realized was out there. How easy it all was. How scary that it was so easy, although the fear was part of the fun, that edge of danger that made it so delicious. Did Mish do this all the time? She seemed to know how to get liquor, and she'd done poppers before. What else did she do?

Mish flicked her cigarette on the ground. "Okay, thanks, see you around."

"Hey, you can't just leave," said Arnold.

"Why not?" said Mish, jutting out her chin.

"Told you I would collect," he said.

"Well, what do you want?" said Mish, hands on hips.

Arnold pretended to think on it. "How about a kiss?" he suggested.

Mish screwed her face. "Ew! Never!" Mish had a boyfriend. She didn't have to put up with this kind of thing from Arnold, the neighborhood loser.

But Leo was already leaning toward him. She couldn't see clearly, she was high, this was fun, Arnold was fun, he was a friend, and all he wanted was a kiss. She could do that. Why not?

"I'll kiss you," she offered.

Mish wrinkled her nose, obviously opposed to the idea. "Ew, no! Don't kiss him! We don't owe him anything!"

But Arnold was already leaning over, and Leo leaned closer as well. She closed her eyes, prepared for a full tongue bath, but he gave her only a peck on the lips.

"That wasn't too bad, right?" he said with a smile. "So, Sparkle?"

Mish once again looked repulsed. "You're not coming."

Arnold slung an arm around Leo's shoulders. "I think that's for the birthday girl to decide, don't you think?"

What could it hurt? Arnold had given them drugs for free. Mish had her boyfriend, so why couldn't Arnold come with them? Was Mish embarrassed to be seen with two people from Woods Forest Park? Screw that.

Leo put her arm around Arnold's waist. "The birthday girl says Arnold's welcome."

FIFTEEN

Exes and Ohs, Part One

October 19
The Present
8:45 P.M.

As Montserrat walked away, smug with the knowledge that she knew what was going on with Sam while Ellie didn't, Ellie was struck by another fear. One that had never occurred to her before. Did Montserrat know what was going on with Sam because she was still sleeping with Todd? Was Todd cheating on her with his hot ex-wife?

Everyone cheats. That's what her mother believed and so that's what Ellie believed. Before her dad went to jail, he hadn't been faithful, her mom said. It was just the way it was. Like the lights going out if there was no money to pay the electric bill, or the way they made do with a dinner of hot dogs and crackers when the food stamps ran out.

Everyone cheats, no one is faithful, no one is good, the world is cruel, the universe indifferent, and your husband will sleep with someone else in time.

Everyone cheats. Half her friends in LA were cheaters. They all had affairs. London and New York, not so much. What was the difference? Ellie wondered. Were the LA people just more attractive and hence had more opportunity? Possibly. Archer's group of aristocrats were a somewhat shabby bunch. Sure, they owned vineyards in South Africa and threw lavish hunting parties in their country homes, but most of them were total *bow-wows*, snaggletoothed and dandruffy. The richer they were, the more they resembled their dogs. There was a reason Camilla Parker Bowles was nicknamed the Rottweiler. Her New York friends were decidedly more glamorous, but more intent on building their brands, their companies, and ferrying their children from one status-signifying extracurricular activity to another. They were too busy to have sex with *anyone*.

Still, everyone cheats. Ellie had been a guest at an engagement party for one of her model friends, and the talk of the night was that Cosima was annoyed that Kate Moss was coming to her wedding because it turned out Kate Moss was her fiancé's mistress.

"So what's the big deal? So Marcus fucks Kate once in a while, *everyone* fucks Kate," the bride was told. Go on with the wedding. So he's a cheater. So he cheats on you with Kate Moss. At least she's famous. Europeans were so blasé.

Americans felt guiltier about infidelity, but they still did it.

Ellie scanned the room, knowing half the couples were keeping secrets from each other. There was the beautiful soap star cheating on her husband with their eighteen-year-old manny, while her husband, the producer of the show, was cheating with his assistant. Over by the piano, there was the magazine executive who spent half her time traveling with her "work husband," who took that title literally—they even booked the same rooms on every trip. Meanwhile, her *husband* husband had a new skank on his arm at Soho House every night. There was Todd's sister-in-law, who'd gone to Rome on an artists' retreat and slept with the eighteen-year-old nephew of the artist. Todd's brother was still married to her—why, Ellie didn't know. Maybe he was just biding his time to hook up with his own eighteen-year-old, if he hadn't already. When her friends caught their husbands cheating, they didn't even divorce them; usually they just embarked on revenge affairs. Divorce was messy—a drain on the lifestyle and the cash flow, plus there were the kids to think about. A revenge affair was much more efficient.

Everyone cheats. It was depressing.

Didn't people make promises when they got married? Vows? Forsaking all others, to love and to cherish, till death do us part? Didn't she promise that? Didn't Todd? Ellie can't remember their vows. The guy who married them in St. Barts had a thick French accent; who knows what he asked of them? She was pretty bombed when they walked out to the beach, so drunk she could hardly keep the dress on her shoulders, and the baby was crying.

They'd met at a party in Brooklyn, of all places, at one of those humongous loft parties in Dumbo thrown by the hippest people you know, when Brooklyn was finally the place to be instead of the place no one ever wanted to go because you could never get a taxi back to Manhattan. It was before Uber, practically prehistoric. It was ten years ago, when she'd just moved back to New York again from London. She and Archer had tried to work things out for the sake of the baby, but neither of them had that kind of self-sacrifice in them. Archer was Archer. He was there for her all the way up from conception to the birth. But after the baby was born, Archer was back to his old habits, hitting Annabel's and leaving for Spain for the weekend while she had to stay home and take care of the squalling bundle of joy. If she was going to be alone, Ellie decided she'd much rather be alone in New York.

People (therapists, her best friends, Todd) said she had daddy issues, but she never knew her dad long enough to be hurt by his absence or his negligence. So how could she have issues if she never even related to having a father? Archer was more a baby than a father figure. Even when she was seventeen and started dating him, she had to take care of *him*, not the other way around. Sure, he paid for everything, duh, but she did everything else.

Anyway, Todd. He was at that loft party, and still wearing a wedding ring. Technically, of course, he was still married, but they were separated, he told her. They were living apart. His wife had moved out and had a new boyfriend—some real estate guy. Todd had showed her pictures of his kid—gap-toothed Sam— and she had shown him photos of baby Giggy. She told him she was divorced, which was the truth. They had filed papers before she'd left, but they weren't finalized yet.

Todd was such a star back then. He'd just come back from Rockefeller Center for the network upfronts. At the party in Brooklyn, Ellie remembered, all those young starlets clustered around him, pressing their tits against his elbow. But he'd only had eyes for her.

Sure, Ellie had gotten around. She went through a bit of a slutty phase. She'd slept with a lot of famous people. She was a model, come on. Rock stars. Rap stars. Actors. It was something to do. Later, she would see them on television or on the movie screen and she'd laugh, remembering which one couldn't finish, which one had a pencil dick, which one had cried afterward. But she'd never truly fallen in love. Not like this. Okay, so maybe Archer, twenty years older, had been a sort of daddy after all. She loved Archer, but she'd fallen in love with Todd. There was a difference.

Todd was a daddy, but he wasn't her daddy.

Todd was only five years older than her.

When they met, he was thirty-five, not even forty, but he was a dad with a kid, and Ellie was just over thirty with a baby already. A single dad and a single mom. She was feeling bloated and ugly and her boobs were leaking. But that night she'd worn her usual tank top without a bra and her torn jeans and her shitkicker boots, and her hair was a blond tangle down her back. She looked like the kind of girl who graced every car commercial and hamburger ad in America and when he looked over at her, past the overdressed starlets, she'd smiled at him.

"Let's get out of here," he'd said, a hand on her back. So confident, so sure. She can't even remember what she'd said or did that made him think she would leave with him right then, but she did. She had live-in help, and a night nurse giving Giggy her 2:00 A.M. bottle.

They went back to his hotel room and fucked all night. His penis was huge. What did they call it now? Big Dick Energy, yeah, exactly. She had to smile just thinking about it. She'd told all her gays the next day at brunch, holding up her hands spaced widely apart. It was like she'd won the lottery.

Was Todd cheating on Montserrat back then when he'd slept with Ellie? When he'd taken her back to his hotel room? Was he cheating if he was still wearing a wedding ring? Was he cheating if he was only separated, not divorced?

Was *she* the other woman?

Ellie had never slept with a married man. Never. It was another of her rules. No married guys. Had he lied to her about being separated?

No, because when she flew out to Los Angeles the next weekend, Todd was living in an apartment above Sunset. He'd been there for a while; it was decorated—rugs on the floor, art on the walls. There was a little bedroom for his kid, Sam, who lived with him every other week; they traded custody.

When Ellie met Todd, Montserrat was already living in a penthouse on Wilshire with her boyfriend. Ellie had seen the photos of them online. Montserrat had traded Todd for some real estate mogul, much older and swarthier but with a much fatter bank account. But try reminding Montserrat about that, because when she found out Todd wasn't coming back to her, she was *livid*. When the boyfriend dumped her, she wanted her husband back, except he didn't want her back anymore. Todd had moved on, to Ellie, to Giggy, the four of them with Sam in tow, doing all the dorky family things. Ellie left New York and the four of them had settled into a five-bedroom Spanish colonial in Brentwood. They'd even gotten a dog together—their pouty little Maltese puppy, Cece. Ugh—that was another problem—Ellie had completely forgotten about the Cece issue. She still had to tell Todd about it. Crap.

Todd paid Montserrat off with Ellie's money, and the minute his divorce was final, they hightailed it to St. Barts and made it official. No prenup, even if Ellie's company was flying high. What was she thinking? She was in love and Todd had his own money. She'd had to sign a prenup when she married Archer, but there was land in Surrey and in the South of France, unbreakable trusts that had been set up for his children, for Giggy.

So: Was Todd cheating on his wife with her back then? Ellie weighed all the facts and decided no. He was truly separated from Montserrat and their marriage was over.

But was he cheating on Ellie with his ex-wife *now*? Had the tables turned?

Todd and Montserrat had become chummy lately. They were positively affectionate these days, sharing laughs about Sam. During Sam's high school graduation, everyone assumed *they* were still a couple, they presented such a united front—the proud parents. Ellie was just the stepmonster, just the one who'd paid all the bills for that fancy private school and the private SAT tutoring and the elite summer camps, yeah.

Todd would be insane if he was sleeping with Montserrat. He couldn't be. He couldn't be sleeping with her. Montserrat was toxic. No matter that she was a serene yoga goddess now, she had the heart of a viper and Todd wasn't dumb. He wouldn't go back there.

But just because he wasn't fucking his ex-wife didn't mean he wasn't fucking someone else.

But who?

Who was he fucking?

But didn't Ellie have bigger things to worry about right now? Like the fact that *he* was coming to the party?

Talk about an ex.

She'd *ex'd* him out of her life.

What did he want? Why was he coming over? Did he want to talk about that night? That night that they never, ever, ever talked about—the night when . . .

Ellie shook her head. She didn't want to remember. Maybe, hopefully, he wouldn't show up at all. But when had she ever been that lucky?

SIXTEEN

Exes and Ohs, Part Two

October 19
The Present
9:00 P.M.

Todd downed the rest of his drink and kept his gaze upon the strange man in their backyard. Ellie swore she had no idea who he was, but Todd had learned not to believe everything his wife said. Oh, not that she was lying per se, but she often didn't want him to know exactly what she was up to, and he had a strong feeling that Ellie wasn't telling him the entire truth. Not about that guy, nor how much the party cost, nor exactly how much money she had borrowed from the bank. He knew they were deeply in debt, and buying this house two months ago hadn't helped, but it wasn't as if he could stop her either, it wasn't as if she ever listened to him. Her label was floundering, that much he knew, since she was always complaining about their weak social media presence and how they couldn't compete with all the new internet-based clothing companies with no overhead and brick-and-mortar expenses.

He was vaguely aware that their entire enterprise was a literal house of cards that could crash down at any moment, but he didn't know exactly how bad it was, and he wished he did. He wished she would lean on him a little more, let him in, but they'd been estranged for so long and they'd gotten used to living with the tension. He'd been depressed and withdrawn, and she'd thrown herself headfirst into saving her company, so there was little time for intimacy, let alone decent conversation.

"Todd!" came a honeyed, patrician voice that could only belong to his wife's ex-husband.

Lord Fauntleroy! he'd almost said, but bit it back. "Archer!" he said, slapping the tall, red-faced Brit on the back. "How are you, man? Good to see you!" he said, without an ounce of sincerity. He wasn't jealous of Archer, who was old and graying and had a paunch and, honestly, was a bit pathetic with all the skirt chasing at his age. But the fact that the old coot had known Ellie first, yeah, that still grated.

"Everything good?" he said, hoping he could get rid of him as soon as possible.

"Good, good," said Archer affably. "You?"

"Can't complain," said Todd, who had a lot to complain about, including the end of his television career, the twenty pounds he'd gained from the stress (not fifty; Ellie always exaggerated), his wife's manic overspending, and the mystery of why his eldest daughter had suddenly come home from college. "Did you and Giggy have a nice weekend?"

"Lovely," said Archer.

Whenever Archer blew into town, they had to force his daughter to spend time with him, which she hated. It gave Todd a certain satisfaction. Giggy had reluctantly spent the weekend with Archer at his hotel with his newest girlfriend, and had returned home with more complaints.

"He's embarrassing!" Giggy had told him while they ate ice cream in the kitchen together. "He doesn't know how to work the TV remote in the hotel, so he's always calling for someone to do it, even at three in the morning, which wakes me up even in the other room because the walls in the suite are so thin. He's a child," said their ten-year-old child.

She detailed the rest of her grievances: Archer couldn't find his eyeglasses and so had to have someone from the hotel read the selections to him, which took so long that he decided he wasn't hungry after all, so Giggy didn't get breakfast; Archer invited a few of his girlfriend's friends over and they had a loud party in the suite and she couldn't sleep.

"At least we're not in LA," said Giggy.

"Why? What happens in LA?"

"He can't drive, so he takes me to school in an Uber, which isn't allowed on campus, and the guard always stops us at the gate, which makes everyone beep," she whined.

Privately, Todd wished that Ellie would put her foot down with Archer and tell Giggy she didn't have to see him. Giggy didn't even like to be called Giggy anymore—she preferred Imogen, barely. "What kind of stupid name did I get?" she'd say, scowling.

"It's British," Ellie would explain. "You're British."

Giggy refused to believe it.

After eating her ice cream, Giggy was back to running around the party with her little friend Zoe, ignoring the mean triumvirate this time. The twins were once more causing havoc in the playroom, now that the lesser DJ had absconded. But where was Samantha? Where was his eldest child? Why was she home all of a sudden?

Oh, wait. He knew why she was home, didn't he? Didn't she mention something when she'd texted him a week or so ago— some kind of thing at school? But he had been too busy to pay attention, and it was Sam after all—she'd never gotten into any kind of trouble before, had been the model child, so well behaved, studious, and diligent, so he hadn't even really believed it. What was it? There was a scandal of some sort, with a professor of hers, about a paper she'd plagiarized. Wait, what? How could their perfect eldest child be accused of plagiarism of all the insane things? Was he remembering correctly?

"Hey, Otis," he said, spying the younger twin (even if he was only two minutes younger, he would always be the "younger twin" for the rest of his life) barreling out of the game room, holding a Super Soaker. Oh boy. Todd had to give the twins props; they never gave up on causing mayhem.

"Have you seen your sister?"

Otis grinned, his mouth red from the Popsicles Todd had allowed them earlier, and pointed at Giggy, who was now blowing bubbles by the pool.

"No, not that one. Sam? Have you seen Sam?"

"Sam's here?" Otis asked, jumping up in excitement. "Where's Sam?"

"That's what I was asking you—oh, forget it," said Todd. "And give me that! Don't wet the guests!" He grabbed the water pistol from his boy's hands and handed it to the party planner, denying the child for the first time that evening. "Put that somewhere he can't find it, will you?"

"Of course," said Madison Lexington (Todd joked she was an intersection until Ellie corrected him and said those two avenues actually didn't meet). The poor woman had two distinct lines on her otherwise frozen forehead, probably because she couldn't satisfy any of Ellie's demands quickly enough.

Todd looked over the party to see if he could find his eldest daughter and instead found the couple Ellie had wanted kicked out.

Had Melvin really brought a hooker? And, if so, how much did she cost? He was merely curious, not interested. When they'd first gotten married, Ellie had been wary, if not downright paranoid, that Todd would remain faithful to her, given the parade of actresses and wannabe actresses throwing themselves at him, Mr. Network President.

Sure, he'd had his fun over the years before he met Ellie, had his share of girlfriends, hookups, one-night stands, but here was the thing that he kept telling her, kept trying to make her believe—actually, it was not that fun. It was not fun knowing they liked you only for what you could do for them. Yes, he'd been surrounded by pretty girls, the prettiest girls from all their small towns. They all ended up in Los Angeles, all vying for the same tiny number of roles, all desperate for stardom. All willing to do whatever it took to land the part, except he was never interested in the casting couch, never took anyone up on that kind of offer. He was not a transactional guy. His girlfriends were agents and executives, friends of friends from business school. Sure, the occasional actress, but he was careful never to date anyone employed by his studio. It was such a cliché, and all those pretty girls—not all of them could or would be stars—most of them ended up in real estate if they were lucky, and if they were not, porn. The Valley, after all, was only a few exits away from Hollywood, and it was just another studio.

He could have dated the hottie of the week, but he found the girls boring, vacuous to the point of stupid, and always working. Sure, he was a bit of a snob. He'd always been a smart, good-looking guy, not the kind of nerd who suddenly dated bombshells, even though he had his share of attention. Now that he was nobody, it was almost a relief at first. He remembered when people craned their necks to see him, when they hung on his every word, and it initially felt liberating to be free of the pressure. But now he was like a ghost; sometimes he wasn't even sure if people noticed he was there. He'd mourned a little, but it wasn't so much the attention he missed as much as his old identity.

He'd worked for the network for almost twenty years, working his way up from production assistant to line producer to executive producer to executive vice president to president of the whole shebang! He called the shots, decided on which shows to put on the air, and the town prostrated themselves at his feet. He hadn't made it as an actor, but he still looked like one. He was proud and, like Ellie, he'd come from nothing—he too was a poor kid from a podunk town, but his route was through Harvard and Harvard Business School to the top of the ranks.

Then, disaster.

Streaming services grew in popularity and the network began

to flail, loss of audience leading to loss of ad dollars and finally to loss of faith. His boss explained it was time for a change, new blood at the helm, someone who could get the eyeballs of those kids who spent more time on their phones and tablets than watching network television.

So Todd was out. And some young buck was in.

Whatever. He was done with TV anyway, and he certainly didn't want his kids anywhere near the industry. None of the executives ever did; it was agreed among them that it was the absolute worst environment for a child. It wasn't that the stories were true about Hollywood pedophile rings, at least not as far as he knew. Todd had no idea if it was truly as skeevy as the rumors said—the grotto parties and the rent boys and the abuse and the suicides. All he knew was that he had never seen it himself. He steered clear of those directors, those producers who wafted around with whispers about their clandestine behavior. He avoided them.

But he knew enough about how the industry worked to know he didn't want his kids anywhere near it. He'd seen network executives make fun of kids' looks, of their weight. He'd been one of those executives on the phone with the stage moms, berating them for their offspring's tabloid antics. When a certain child star transitioned from moon-faced cherub to nearly naked cover star, he was the one who'd had to send the angry email to her parents. But he was also the one who okayed the tiny miniskirts on the show, clothes he'd never let his teenage daughter wear.

Hollywood was a caste system, with the wannabes on one side who would let their kids do anything to land a role, book a gig, while the insiders were on the other, and *their* children were spe-

cial. Their children didn't have to work to put food on the table,
their children went to private schools and starred in school plays,
and when they were good and ready, they could be cast in a film
if they chose to pursue acting, but only after they'd graduated
from high school and only if Steven was directing (Spielberg of
course.) Otherwise, their kids went to Stanford, or Harvard, or
Columbia, or USC, and if they worked in entertainment, they
were producers or executives. There were exceptions of course—
there always were, but the exceptions proved the rule.

They'd done all right with Sam, and he figured whatever was
wrong, they'd be able to fix it. Sam was a good kid. They'd been
lucky with all their kids. If only Ellie could see that, if only it was
enough. They didn't need all this and they certainly didn't need
this fancy party they couldn't afford.

He circled the backyard, having lost sight of the strange man.
Luckily, no one stopped to make small talk. Well, they were mostly
Ellie's friends, and he'd already had a dozen casual conversations
with most of them all weekend. He was running out of chitchat.
There were too many people he didn't recognize. His head hurt.

What time was it? He saw Ellie by the bar and, without thinking, grabbed her phone out of her hand to check the time. She was
deep in conversation with a friend from London, so didn't notice
a text had arrived on her home screen. Ellie tended to lose sight of
anything in the presence of her old gay boyfriend, Blake Burberry. She swore nothing had ever happened between them, that
Blake was gay, but Todd had his suspicions.

Todd looked down and read the text.

I'm not leaving. From a number he didn't recognize. He went to the conversation and found the texts she'd sent, his heart sinking with every text bubble.

> Don't do this.
> Don't leave me.
> I need you.

That was it. The rest of the conversation had been deleted, but she hadn't had time to delete this.

His heart began to pound. So he was right. Ellie was having an affair. She had to be. She was gorgeous, and they hadn't had sex in weeks—months even. And even before then, it had been sporadic. He blamed the network, the stress, the humiliation. He'd lost his mojo, his juice, his will. He'd lost everything. Okay, so maybe he wasn't perfect, maybe he hadn't been the perfect husband all these years, and now he was flawed and sad and depressed and he'd let her down, that was for sure. Guilt pricked his conscience and he tried to shake it away. He didn't want to think about what he'd done.

But now his wife was fucking someone else.

Maybe she was fucking that strange man, the one circling the party on the sidelines, who acted as if he were looking for something—or someone.

Todd deleted the text in a fit of pique and crushed his napkin in his fist. He would find out. Call him out. Call them both out. He wouldn't stand for this. Wouldn't lose her without a fight.

Part Two

THE MAIN COURSE

SEVENTEEN

Dairy Queen(s)

October 19
Twenty-Four Years Ago
9:00 P.M.

It was the first time Leo had stood up to Mish, inviting Arnold to come with them to the club. She didn't notice until then that she always went along with whatever Mish decreed. Arnold grinned. "The birthday girl says I can come with, so I'll see you ladies there."

"You're not coming with us right now?" asked Leo, a little deflated.

"Naw, I got some more work to do, but I'll catch you guys there, okay?" he said, looking apologetic. He pulled his baseball cap down low.

"Yeah, we'll see you, Arnold," said Mish sarcastically, rolling her eyes to the heavens.

Arnold saluted them and shuffled off, disappearing into the alley once again.

"I can't believe you said he could join us!" said Mish, as they stomped back to the car to fetch Brooks before going to the club.

"Why can't he? He's nice," said Leo. "What's the big deal?"

"It's just . . ." Mish said, shrugging. "I mean, you can do so much better is all."

"Like your rich preppy boyfriend, you mean?" said Leo. She held her breath, thinking she had crossed a line, but Mish only nodded.

"Exactly," said Mish. "I mean you *kissed* him. Gross."

They walked the rest of the way back to the car in silence, but there was something new between them. Leo felt betrayed, and Mish was irritated.

When they got to the car, Brooks was waking up. "Where'd you guys go?" he asked, rubbing his eyes.

"Out," said Mish. She held up the little bottle. "For the club. Later."

"Sweet," said Brooks. "I'm hungry. Is anyone else starving?"

Mish looked at her watch. "Well, we still have a little time. Dairy Queen?"

"Yum," said Brooks. "Dairy Queen."

"We're really showing Brooks a classy time, aren't we?" said Leo in a snide tone. Her irritation with Mish had sobered her up.

"Everyone goes to Dairy Queen," said Mish.

"That's not true," said Leo. "Only poor people do. Brooks, have you ever been?"

Brooks looked sheepish. "I mean, I guess it's kind of far from my house."

"See!" said Leo triumphantly.

"Whatever!" huffed Mish.

Dairy Queen was in a scarier part of the city, and even Leo and Mish didn't know exactly where they were. Brooks had sobered up enough so that he drove them, but he lost a little of his bravado as they drove past boarded-up buildings and abandoned warehouses, the streets empty except for homeless people and junkies.

Leo's mother never cooked; she had that in common with Mish's mom. On the rare occasions that she was home for dinner, she only made mashed potatoes from a box, which was the one thing she knew how to cook. When Leo was in elementary school, she was eligible for reduced lunch, and so she would always walk up to the cashier and give her a dime and say, "Reduced," but then, so did Mish. Their elementary school was small and almost all the kids were on the government meal plan. There were days that school lunch was the only meal she ate. That was before her mom found a steady job at the restaurant.

But now that they were in high school, they noticed that not everyone was on the reduced plan; in fact, most of the kids they went to school with were not. So now it mattered, and since it mattered, they chose not to eat in the cafeteria. Instead, they ate a lot of fast food, the cheaper the better. Maybe that was why she'd gained all that weight that the modeling lady told her to lose.

"Drive through or eat in?" asked Brooks.

"Drive," said Leo.

"Eat in," said Mish. "You don't want your car to stink."

"Right," said Brooks.

———

They walked inside, feeling self-conscious; the crowd was sleazy and poor, bordering on homeless, but at least they were with Brooks, who walked confidently to the counter. He paid for a few burgers and Blizzards and they slid into a booth to eat them. Mish squeezed in next to Brooks, but the table was so small that even if Leo was across from them, her knees were knocking against his. She pretended not to notice and so did he.

Mish picked up her burger and took a huge bite. "Yum!"

Leo's stomach was loudly complaining, but she picked at hers, wanting Brooks to notice how different she was from his girl-friend, how she was that much more refined. So what if the only guy interested in her was the corner drug dealer. It didn't mean Mish was better than her.

She never asked for this, she didn't want to be sitting under-neath this fluorescent light, eating burgers made with prison-grade meat on her birthday. She thought longingly of home, and the Carvel cake, but it was only nine o'clock; there was no way her mom would be home.

Mish and Brooks were doing that happy couple thing where he was feeding her fries and she was tucked underneath his arm, giggling, stealing kisses between bites. The sight of the two of them made her sick. She pushed her food away.

"Not hungry?" asked Mish.

"No, I lost my appetite," said Leo.

"Maybe you're hungry for something else," said Mish know-ingly.

"Like what?" Leo glared.

"I don't know, you're the one who couldn't wait to run off with Arnold," said Mish.

"Arnold? You guys were with Arnold?" said Brooks, disbelievingly. "That guy is a loser!"

"Leo kissed him," said Mish with a naughty smile.

Leo's cheeks burned but she didn't deny it. Even though it was barely a kiss, more like a brush of his lips against hers. It was nothing. She said so. "It was nothing."

Still, Brooks regarded her with new interest, and there was something like jealousy in his voice. "You and Arnold, huh?"

"Yeah," said Leo. "He's meeting us at the club."

"God, I hope not," said Mish. She could be such a bitch sometimes.

Leo felt something press against her knee. It was Brooks's knee, which had knocked against hers the whole time they were sitting there, but this time, she didn't fidget away, didn't try to fold herself into a smaller space; she let his knee, then his thigh, slide against her knee and her thigh, so that they were pressed together, under the table.

He looked up at her, a curious look in his eyes.

Mish was in his arms, but he was looking right at Leo, and she knew what he was doing. He was picturing her kissing Arnold.

She could see it in his eyes, could see what he was seeing.

He was seeing her. He wanted her. She knew, she always knew when they wanted her. But what she didn't know was what she would do about it.

They finished their meal, and they went to the club.

EIGHTEEN

Dinner Is Served

October 19
The Present
9:05 P.M.

"What's with you?" Ellie asked impatiently. Todd had a weird look on his face but she ignored it for now; she had bigger problems than her husband's unpredictable moods. Was he thinking about Montserrat? Or whatever floozy he was cheating on her with?

He shook his head.

"Can I have my phone back now?" she demanded.

When he didn't respond, she grabbed it out of his hand. He walked away without saying a word to her.

She wanted to call out to him but changed her mind. Men. They were so annoying. If only she could go back in time, go back to before, she still remembered what it was like, being young, before puberty, before the catcalls and the comments and the leers and the groping hands. When she was just a kid, when she was still a *person*, before she became a *girl*. Then suddenly it all changed. She couldn't simply wear tank tops and shorts or even sit the way she used to, spread out like a frog. Suddenly, there were all these rules to follow and she was terrible at rules. Oh, she distinctly remembered what being a teenager was like, more specifically a certain sixteenth birthday, even if she'd spent the rest of her life trying to forget. (But how could she forget the sight of blood on the floor, and the sound of screams. No. No. No. She had to forget. Damn him for texting her, for threatening to come to the party, for walking back into her life like nothing had happened.)

She'd convinced Madison-and-Lex (Todd's clever nickname for their party planner) that they could seat everyone in two long tables in the space between the dining and the living room, right in front of the indoor marble firepit with the newly installed chimney vent. Ellie had insisted on a formal sit-down dinner, and had almost demanded everyone wear white tie. Like at Mean Celine's husband's fortieth, at the Metropolitan Club in New York, or another friend's eighteenth birthday bash for their eldest son, in their twelfth-century palazzo in Venice, complete with fireworks. But she had to be real; this was the desert, and the men were already sweating through their Mr. Turk button-downs and white pants, and the women's colorful Pucci dresses were starting to stick to their thighs. Inside was not any better; even with the air conditioners going full blast, the floor-to-ceiling doors were left completely open for stylish effect. If she had asked them to wear white tie and tails, and ball gowns, everyone would think she was throwing a costume party.

Still, it was gorgeous, and if it was a little crowded, who cared? They could squeeze. The two long tables were set with tall silver candelabras, and the skinny floral arrangements reached almost to the ceiling, the newest trend, instead of the usual fat and squat bouquets—so that you could actually talk to the person sitting across from you instead of trying to crane your neck over the centerpiece. Everything was white—from the flowers to the chairs, to the tablecloths and the napkins, crisp Italian linens embroidered with the Gulf House crest she'd paid a graphic designer to create (a rush order, she had paid a pretty penny to get them in time), and once the sun had set, you couldn't tell the flowers were half-dead in the candlelight.

"Where do we sit?"

"Where do you want us?"

"Who goes where?"

Her friends crowded around her, gushing over the stunning table setting. "Anywhere! Anywhere!" she said, looking pointedly at Blake, who always insisted on place cards, even for small dinner parties, and had once sat Todd next to someone's nanny, who had a place at a table with a ten-month-old baby. Blake had had a brief career as an ersatz reality television producer, and Todd as network president had rejected all his pilot pitches, so Blake doled out his revenge through his seating order. Todd refused ever to attend one of Blake's events again.

"You should sit at the head," said Sanjay. "You're the birthday girl."

"No, no, no," said Ellie. "You sit there." Now that the evening was in full swing, she was abashed at all the effort and expense it had taken to get to this point, and she wanted nothing more than to hide. She chose a seat in the middle of the row, between one half of the tangential couples they barely knew from the kids' schools and an old friend from the garment trade.

All weekend long, Ellie had wanted people to notice her, for her life to incite envy and admiration, but now that the party was under way, she felt too exposed, as if she had shown too much, had revealed too much of herself, her ambition, her desires. She had orchestrated this nine-course banquet, but now her heels hurt and she wished everyone would leave so her family could run out and grab burgers and shakes at McDonald's.

But whatever! They were sitting down to a nine-course meal, inspired by her favorite dishes from Nobu (granted a bit twenty-years-ago, but it was still her favorite restaurant). She had harangued her caterer to make sure she had the correct recipes until the poor woman almost had a nervous breakdown two days before the event.

"Oh, how fun," said the woman on her left—one of the moms from Glenwood—as a line of white-gloved attendants walked out of the kitchen, each one bearing a plate covered with a silver dome, and stood behind the chair of each guest. "Was this your idea?"

Ellie nodded, watching as the attendants, with a dramatic flourish, leaned over and served everyone all at once, like a chorus line of backup dancers (which many of them were). Excited murmurs filled the room as the scent of white truffles filled the air. So many fucking truffles! Eighty dollars an ounce and she'd bought *pounds* of it! Ellie knew the price of everything (and the value of everything, ha). Another group of servers positioned themselves behind the guests once more and poured the wine. Only the best white Burgundy, a northern Chablis, chosen expressly for how hard it was to come by in the United States, and no, the servers whispered to anyone who asked, so sorry, there was no red wine to be had, no red wine at all. Never forget the Minotti couch.

Ellie looked down at her plate, pleased, but found she couldn't take a bite. She couldn't eat. She was too full of anxiety and excitement and worry. Why hadn't Harry called her back? He hadn't even texted her back! What was going on with their deal? And where was the photographer from *Vanity Fair*? He was missing everything! She waved Madison over. "Has anyone from the magazine arrived?"

"No, no one." Madison had also acted as the publicist for the party, even though there wasn't supposed to be any publicity since it was a private event. But in the interest of promoting the business, they still had to post everything on Instagram so that their customers would see how amazing Ellie's lifestyle—her *life*—was. "What time were they supposed to be here?"

"Now," said Ellie with a frown. Maybe the editor had changed her mind? It happened. She had come so close on so much good coverage—she was supposed to have a major actress on the cover of *InStyle* wearing a Wild & West dress, but at the last minute, they went with an actor in Ralph Lauren. Then there was the profile in the *New York Times* Style section, but that was killed because the writer had been an old friend and it was "against policy." "So you can't write about any of your old friends? What kind of bullshit is that?" she'd demanded. At a Golden Globes gifting suite last year, she had given a host of starlets wardrobes full of her clothes, with little notes to them, politely asking that if they post, they do so with the correct hashtags. But so far, only some girl no one had ever heard of, on a show no one watched, had posted a picture of herself wearing the free tank top. And the next day, all the Wild & West gift bags were listed on eBay. Bitches!

Starlets, who needed them? she huffed.

"Did you say something?" asked the mom—what was her name?—Chrissy? Kristi? Kristen? No, it was Kirsten. Kirsten, the part-time yoga teacher who was married to one of the founders of the largest video game company in the world.

"No, nothing," said Ellie. "How is your practice?"

"Oh, it's great," said Kirsten, smiling because no one ever remembered what she did since her husband was the one who had the big job. "I'm going to a retreat in Baja later this month."

"I'll come in and take a class sometime," Ellie promised.

"I'd love that! I only teach on Mondays at eleven," said Kirsten.

Ellie smiled. It's not that she hated stay-at-home moms, she despised them. No, that wasn't true—she liked them; some of her best friends were stay-at-home moms! It was the moms who *pretended* to work, who pretended to have something in common with her that she hated. Sorry but no, working one hour a week at a dinky yoga studio for free perks was not the same as running a multimillion-dollar company, fuck you very much. (She should really stop swearing; one of her dearest stay-at-home mom friends had a swear jar. Maybe she should get one, although when she suggested it to her family, Todd laughed and said if they did, they'd be broke by noon.) Why had she invited this insipid faux-spiritual yoga bimbo to her birthday party? Oh, right. Her daughter Zoe was kind to Giggy, who was getting terribly bullied at school. Okay, then.

"Get a load of that one," said Shari, on her right, as she puffed on her vape right in the middle of dinner. "Who's that cute young thing?"

Shari had been a friend since London, Tokyo, and New York. They had been models together, and now Shari ran one of the biggest swimsuit companies in North America. If you swam, if you were ever wet, you wore one of her suits. Shari had a plane and had just closed on her fifth house, located on an island off New Zealand's Northland, where everyone who was anyone was buying these days, for the thinking was that it would be the only country safe from the coming apocalypse.

Ellie looked to where she was pointing. Huh. It was a young, buxom girl that she didn't recognize. There were a few guests she didn't know by name or by face, spouses, plus-ones, but she was certain she'd never seen that girl before. The girl was laughing and biting her lip. And who was she talking to? Oh, wait, was that *Todd*?

Todd was laughing and doing that thing, running his fingers through his dark hair. He was *flirting*.

After all, the girl was pretty, and so young.

Was her husband fucking that girl?

Todd certainly wasn't fucking *her*. They hadn't had sex in what—who knew? Who could remember? If he wasn't with his ex-wife, was he having an affair with that girl? What else could it be?

Then there was *him*. She glanced at her phone, at his texts from earlier in the evening. Happy birthday, girl. See you tonight. He said he would be there, that he would show up later. Almost as a threat. But would he? It had been so long. So many years. Would he even recognize her? Would she recognize him?

Why now? Why was he suddenly reappearing in her life? What did he want?

She remembered that awful night. Did he want money? Was he going to blackmail her? Was that it? They had agreed it was all an *accident*. It was no one's fault. It certainly wasn't her fault. She was just an innocent bystander. Right?

She couldn't eat.

The waiters took away her untouched plate—all those truffles; she should ask them to set it aside for the dog, she thought, even though that spoiled little Maltese had caused her so much trouble already—when out of the corner of her eye, she saw her husband get up from his seat, leaving the cute girl behind to approach the stranger they'd noticed earlier in the backyard. She'd been honest when he'd asked about the strange man earlier. She had absolutely no idea who he was.

Who was he? He was lingering by the doorway, staring at the party. Every seat was taken and yet there he stood, alone and out of place. She began to have a terrible feeling about this.

She pushed her chair back and ran to the front of the room, right behind her husband. Todd was standing at the doorway, in front of the strange man.

"Can I help you?" he asked. "Are you sure you're in the right place?"

Ellie walked up, and Todd swiveled, his face was getting red. "Ellie, do you know this guy?" he asked in an accusatory tone.

"No! I told you! I have no idea who he is!"

"Mrs. Todd Stinson?" the man asked.

"Yes, that's me."

The man handed Ellie an envelope. "You've been served."

NINETEEN

Dancing Queens (16)

October 19
Twenty-Four Years Ago
10:00 P.M.

Just as Mish had predicted, entrance to the club was easy. No one even checked for IDs. They paid the five-dollar cover and walked inside. The first thing Leo noticed was the stench. It smelled like beer and urine and grime, with a toxic layer of smoke. Leo decided the overpowering smell of smoke was preferable to the stink underneath. There was a crowd in front of the stage, dancing, as the first band played through their set. The music was loud, deafening, but there was a frenetic energy to the place, a sense of mass celebration, and Leo suddenly understood why people gathered at these places. It was a ritual, an offering, a way of marking the weekend, with music, drinks, and laughter.

Brooks had thought to hide the beers in his backpack, so they huddled to a corner where the bartenders and security wouldn't see, and they drank them. Leo's was a little lukewarm, but it was okay. So this was what a nightclub was like. She felt grown up, so much older than when the night had begun. She'd been drunk, then sober, then high, and now she was here. Someone handed her a cigarette, so she smoked it.

"Let's go to the other rooms," said Mish.

"There are more rooms?"

"Duh," said Mish, who, to Leo's surprise, seemed to have been here before, many times. She grabbed Brooks's hand and led them out of the main floor.

The club was made up of a warren of rooms; some were just rooms covered in garish paint, and people were sitting there, drinking and talking, and some were huge rooms with different kinds of music, and people dancing. Mish led them through each room, but she would shake her head and move on, dissatisfied, until they reached a back room that was almost completely dark, with a throbbing bass line and a packed crowd of people dancing in the middle of it. A few girls were dancing on little tables, letting everyone take a good look at them.

"This one," said Mish with a naughty smile, pulling them into the middle of the swaying crowd. Brooks shrugged and moved from side to side, his approximation of dancing.

They danced for a bit, until Mish jumped up on one of the tables and pulled Leo up to dance with her. They danced in sync, and Mish began to gyrate her hips against hers, and Leo ground back, letting Mish's hands move up and down over her body. She did the same.

Mish turned so that she faced Leo. They were almost the same height; it was strange to realize that, when Leo always felt so much bigger than Mish but she actually wasn't. They were the same. People were always saying how much they looked alike. She was looking right into Mish's eyes. Mish pulled her closer and closer, her eyes were glazed, and up close, Leo could see the sparkles in Mish's eye shadow; they glinted in the light. Below them, Brooks took a pull from his beer and watched.

Mish put her hands on either side of Leo's face. She did that sometimes, right before yelling at her to Stop Being So Uptight or Have Some Fun Already. But this time she didn't yell. She just brushed Leo's cheeks softly with her fingertips in a gentle caress.

Then she turned away, and continued to dance. Brooks removed a few more beers from his backpack.

They danced for a few more songs, but Leo got tired of that. Her feet hurt. "I'm going to look for Arnold!" she yelled into Mish's ear so that her friend could hear her over the music.

Mish made a face. Why was she so annoyed with Arnold? Wasn't Arnold an old friend of Mish's? Was she just annoyed Arnold was paying attention to her and not Mish for a change?

"Fine, go, look for him, what do I care? I'm only your best friend, but if you want to hang out with him on your birthday, fine," said Mish, pushing her off the table.

"Don't leave without me," Leo warned.

Mish rolled her eyes. As if.

Leo left her with Brooks, and went to see if she could find her friend.

The club was a maze, staircases going to dark caverns guarded by beefy bodyguards checking for the right wristbands that allowed access to the right VIP rooms, none of which she had. It was hard to see through the smoke and the crowd, but she tried. For a while she worried she'd lost track of time and her friends, and wondered how she would get home—she didn't have enough money for a cab, but she thought she could walk maybe, or call her mom at the restaurant, although that wouldn't be any fun. Which room was the one Mish and Brooks were in? They all looked the same to her, and for a minute, Leo panicked. She was all alone in a crowd of strangers, and she felt very young all of a sudden.

"THERE YOU ARE!"

A hand reached out of the crowd, on the dance floor, and grabbed her head, the fingers clasping around her skull.

She shrank from it at first, but when she looked up, the hand was attached to an arm and the arm was Arnold's. He was grinning.

"Hey!"

"Hey," he said. "Sorry, didn't mean to scare you."

"You didn't," she assured him.

"Where's your posse?"

She shrugged. "Somewhere."

"Mish doesn't like me much," he said.

"Who cares about Mish."

"Come on," he said, and pulled her from the dance floor. He took her to a ledge away from the speakers, where it was quieter. "This is where I work. Want some more?" he asked, handing her a vial. Arnold was the house dealer. Every nightclub had one, or several, to service the patrons who came to party.

She took it and snorted it.

"Cover it with your hands. I mean, girl, come on now."

"Oh, sorry," she said, laughing.

"You're all right."

"Do you work here every night?"

"Some weekends, kind of dead the rest of the week, and I gotta take turns with the other dealers," he explained. He kept his back-pack nearby. Leo understood that's where he kept the drugs.

They talked a little, and once in a while someone would come up to them.

"What you got?" they'd ask.

Arnold would tell them.

Then Arnold would tell them to meet him by the water foun-tain, and he would slip them whatever they asked for and stuff the cash in his back pocket.

Leo leaned back on the wall, affected a bored pose. Sometimes people asked her too. "You got smokes? Uppers? Blues?"

She'd nod over to Arnold.

She felt useful, like she belonged. No one looked at her twice. No one questioned her.

Arnold came back. "I like this song," he said, when the music changed.

"Want to dance?" she asked him.

"Nah, I suck at dancing." He looked a little sad. "Sorry."

"It's all right," she said. And it was.

TWENTY

Pianos and Sopranos

October 19
The Present
10:00 P.M.

Thankfully, Todd didn't make a scene in front of the guests. Instead, he'd looked almost relieved, like it wasn't the worst news in the world, that she was being slapped with a lawsuit. She confessed, told him everything, how their neighbor was suing, of all things, for dog doo-doo. "It was just a misunderstanding," she said. "Well, it began that way, and then they caught it on their camera."

"What happened?"

What happened was that a few months ago, Miranda, their nanny, had called in sick, and Miranda, in addition to shepherding Eli and Otis to their various after-school activities (karate, art, flag football, fencing, and therapy), also took care of the family dog. She was responsible for walking and feeding their rather petulant and overweight Maltese, Cece. Since it was Lynn the LA housekeeper's day off, there was no one else to walk Cece, so Ellie had hired one of those dog-walking services to take Cece around the block.

"You know, since I always have to do everything around here," she said.

Todd frowned and Ellie quickly reversed course. "Sorry, I meant, the burden of day-to-day household management *often* falls to me, even though you are the one at home." She was supposed to stop using the word *always* in their marriage; they had paid an expensive shrink thousands of dollars to tell them this.

Todd shrugged and didn't seem up to the task of defending his right to play video games on his phone all day, so she went on.

"Anyway, I called the service to walk Cece, and this kid took her around the block, picked up the poop, and deposited it in the Andersons' garbage cans because it was trash day and their cans were out and no one had taken ours out yet."

"So?"

"So the Andersons caught it on their security cameras, and they've been harassing us ever since, about how we'd used their garbage cans for Cece's poop, and I guess that's a crime or something? They left notes under the door and voice mails on my phone, but I was so busy I forgot about it and now they're suing us."

Todd barked a laugh. "They're suing us?"

"Well, one night late at work, I kind of called and told them their cameras were trained on our driveway and it was invasion of our privacy and *I* would sue them."

"And?"

Ellie sighed. "I also told Miranda when she came back to work that when she takes Cece out for a walk to make sure Cece pees on their hedges. They caught that on camera too."

Honestly, she explained to him, it wasn't even the worst bad-neighbor lawsuit in the world; according to their lawyer, there was much, much worse. There was a case of two homeowners fighting over beachfront property in Cape Cod, and the bad blood was so bad that one of them never got to build their beach house on their land for twenty-five years. The poor schmuck bought the land to build a dream home for his family, but he and his neighbor sued each other for so many years that he was already divorced and his kids grown and still he didn't have a beach house. Then there was the Saudi prince who's trying to build his five-building mega compound in Benedict Canyon but has been hit with lawsuits from his appalled neighbors, who've been winning their case, forcing the prince to downsize from ninety thousand square feet to a mere sixty thousand.

But yes, this lawsuit was extremely petty, and it was a headache, and on top of everything else going wrong in her life, she was also feuding with their neighbors. She braced herself because now her husband was going to lose his temper because he always—no, often! Often!—blew his top, because that's what Todd was like now that he was bitter and unemployed.

Instead, Todd just shrugged. "Oh," he said. "That's it?"

"*Oh?* That's all you can say?"

He patted her shoulder. "David will take care of it. That's why we have that umbrella policy." David was their lawyer and business manager.

She couldn't quite believe her ears. "Really?"

"Yeah."

"Todd, they're suing us for seven hundred thousand dollars! For dog poop!"

"We have insurance." He shrugged. "They'll probably settle."

"You're not mad?"

"Well, it's too late now, isn't it? To walk the dog ourselves? I mean, come on, we never do that. When was the last time either of us walked Cece?" He looked amused, which was uncharacteristic of him. Todd was usually the one who went ballistic over this sort of thing.

Ellie scratched her cheek. "I guess."

"It'll be fine. We'll get through it. Let the lawyers sort it out. In the meantime, stop calling them and leaving threatening voice mails, and tell Miranda to stop letting Cece pee on their yard."

"Okay," she said, relieved, even if she couldn't bring herself to tell him that she hadn't paid the insurance premium last month, so most likely they *didn't* have insurance to cover it. But that was a conversation for later. For now, she was just glad he wasn't in the mood to quarrel.

"We'll get through it."

"We will?" Her mind was whirling with doubt.

"Yeah, we always do," he said, looking a bit hurt. "But come on, the show's about to start."

Ellie had decided that, between courses, they would have entertainment. Maybe she'd gotten the idea for the pianist from her teenage memories of Nordstrom? She'd also hired an opera singer, maybe because she watched too many Woody Allen movies. Not that she could exactly name one where an opera singer performed, and to be honest, she was just trying to impress the New Yorkers. And also because Mean Celine's childhood friend was a fancy soprano who sang at Mean Celine's husband's white-tie fortieth, and Ellie had been jealous of that moment, which felt so special. Thankfully, Ellie had given enough money to the LA Opera over the years, and the head of the board had persuaded the reigning diva of the company to perform at the party.

They'd installed a piano just for this moment. (No one in the family played; they'd spent thousands of dollars on piano lessons for the kids, and none of them could play a note.)

She tried to catch Todd's eye, but he was seated too far away and talking to Mean Celine's husband, who was probably giving him pointers on how to have an affair. It was old news within their circle that Simon had a fling with one of the flight attendants who worked on their jet. He'd even installed the skank in her own apartment he paid for, and when Mean Celine found out, she'd gone ballistic. Simon threatened to cut them off—her and the kids both—if she told anyone. Mean Celine, whose father's money was the basis of her husband's success, laughed in his face and told everyone. She would not be humiliated in this manner. Still, she didn't divorce him and they reconciled.

Why had Todd looked so relieved when the process server handed her the papers for the lawsuit? What did he know? And who was that girl he was talking to earlier?

She had to stop worrying about it, and tried to focus on Sterling, who was tapping a knife against his wineglass and trying to get everyone's attention.

"Ellie and Todd asked me to introduce the lovely singer we're about to hear. I've been a fan of Madame since I heard her sing in Montreal. I think Ellie should turn forty more often! It's not every day we get a diva in the desert. (Wink.) Although if you stay for bingo at the Ace later, we'll definitely meet some fabulous queens, not that there aren't many here already, present company definitely included."

The audience tittered. Sterling beamed. "Singing 'Habanera' from *Carmen*, this is quite a treat. Everyone please give a warm welcome to . . ."

The opera singer stepped up to the piano and began to sing. Ellie would tell people that it was from her favorite opera but in truth she had no such thing. It all sounded the same to her. She liked going to the opera only because of the champagne at intermission and to see her name as a donor on the program.

The crowd seemed to love it, though, so that was something; they clapped heartily at the end. Ellie looked around and noticed her stepdaughter had come out of her room finally and joined the party. Sam had showered and brushed her hair, and had changed into one of the newest Wild & West dresses from the collection, a crinkly polyester knockoff of the latest Gucci party dress. On Sam, it looked like the real thing.

"Sam!" she called.

Sam looked guilty as she slunk over to her stepmother.

"Honey, do you need to tell us something?" Ellie asked. "What's going on?" She wanted to point out that Sam had already told Montserrat, so she might as well tell her too, but Ellie knew that was the wrong tactic. Sam would just get defensive and clam up, when she needed her to spill, to gush, to let it all out. "Is it school?"

"Um . . ." Sam said, shifting her weight on each heel and looking like the insecure eight-year-old she'd been when they first met. "Yeah."

"Oh, honey, I'm so sorry to hear that," said Ellie. "You know I never went to college, so I have no idea what it's like, but I'm sure whatever it is, it's not as bad as you think." She took a glug from her wineglass. She'd moved seamlessly from vodka martinis to the white Burgundy, which was just a fancy name for Chardonnay, and she was starting to feel a little light-headed, but there was no excuse not to perform her mothering duties.

Sam gnawed on a fingernail. "Okay, but you need to promise not to get mad. Coz it's pretty bad."

"Okay, I promise."

"I've been on academic probation. If I don't pull my grades up, I can't come back in January."

Ellie almost dropped her wineglass but was too worried about what it would do to the floors, so she held on to the stem. But she could feel the smoke pouring out of her ears. "WHAT!"

"Mom, you promised not to get mad!" Sam whined, sounding just like Otis when he wanted something from the toy store.

"I'm not. I'm not. I'm not mad," Ellie lied. She wasn't mad, she was *furious*. Academic probation? Possibly kicked out in January?

How on earth could Sam have fucked up that badly that she was—horror of horrors—flunking out of Stanford? *This is our eldest, she flunked out of Stanford. This is our child, who got kicked out of Stanford. We never go to Stanford anymore, because Sam got expelled for having terrible grades.* As her gays would say, it was not a cute look.

"But how! What happened? Does Daddy know?" Ellie demanded.

Sam didn't answer the question. Instead, she said, "Um, that's not everything."

"There's more?" Ellie gripped the stem of her wineglass so hard it was in danger of shattering in her hand.

"Yeah, the thing is . . ."

But before Sam could finish her sentence, Ellie's phone rang, and it was an international number. Korea. Mr. Harry Kim. Her investor. She swiped to answer it.

"ELLIE!" yelled Sam. "ARE YOU SERIOUSLY TAKING A CALL RIGHT NOW?"

Oh, so we were back to "Ellie" now, were we? Ellie held up a hand to shush her. "Sam, I'm so, so sorry but I have to take this."

"You always do! You always have to work! This is why I don't tell you ANYTHING!" she said, stomping off and running into a waiter, who had to swivel lest he drop his tray of Victor's undrinkable cocktails on the terrazzo.

Ellie wanted to call after her, but this was too important. She turned up the volume so she could catch every word.

"Harry darling!" she said. "I've been trying to get ahold of you all night!" She pressed the phone to her ear. "What text? What did it say? No, I can't hear you! I'm losing you! Hold on, let me see if I can get a better signal in the other side of the house."

She ran across the grass to the east wing.

But it was too late.

The phone went dead.

She'd alienated her sensitive stepdaughter, and she still didn't know what Harry wanted to say to her. Ellie wanted to throw her phone into the pool, she was so frustrated. But she'd planned this party for a year and she HAD to enjoy it. Because it might just be her last chance to enjoy anything.

TWENTY-ONE

Watch That Scene

October 19
Twenty-Four Years Ago
10:30 P.M.

Leo and Arnold didn't have to find Mish and Brooks; they found them. "There you are," Mish said, her hands on her waist. "We were looking for you everywhere!" She had an accusatory tone in her voice that Leo did not appreciate. Brooks looked a bit embarrassed by the whole thing. "Hey, man," he said to Arnold, who nodded.

"We've just been here the whole time," Leo said. "What's up?"

"Nothing . . . OH FUCK ME!" Mish yelled all of a sudden, and she scooted down, crashing into Leo.

"What? What's going on?"

Mish pointed.

Leo froze.

Mish's dad was standing against the back wall, arms crossed, eyes hooded, surveying the scene, smoking a blunt. "We have to leave. Now," said Mish, agitated.

"Hey, chill," said Arnold. He looked over to where the girls were looking. "Oh, fuck."

"Yeah," Mish said tightly. "Let's go."

"Why?" asked Brooks, who was oblivious to what was happening. "I just opened these bottles."

"I thought this was your night to deal," said Leo.

"Yeah, I did too," said Arnold, his jaw clenched. "But whatever. Let's go."

"Babe? What's going on?" Brooks kept asking.

Leo knew Mish didn't want to explain, didn't want to tell him the truth about her father. That he was at the club because he was dealing, just like Arnold. He was probably the other house dealer. Brooks didn't know that much about Mish other than the fact that she was pretty, and that she was a sophomore. Sure, he knew she lived in a not-so-great part of town, but not what that entailed. And Mish didn't want him to know that the guy standing against the wall of the club, with his tatted arms and greasy hair, who was so far from what his own parents looked like, was actually her father. He was so incredibly different from Donald and Judy Overton, with their fleece vests and hiking boots and dorky secret marital language complete with sickly sweet nicknames.

Mish liked to say the only nicknames her dad ever used were for his collection of firearms. Greta the German Luger, and Rosanne the rifle; oh but he was so clever.

How could Mish explain who that man was, and what he was to her, to someone who came from a loving and stable upper-middle-class household? It was too large an expanse to breach, and too humiliating.

"Let's go, before he sees us," whispered Mish, when Brooks turned away to set the beer bottles on a nearby table. "We can't stay here."

"Yes, let's go," agreed Leo, who didn't look back. "Let's get out of here."

Mish shot her a grateful look. When Brooks returned, she said, "Let's go to Stacey's."

"Really?" said Brooks. "Are you sure?"

"Yeah. Leo, you want to go, right? I mean, the night is young and so are we," said Mish.

Leo turned to Arnold. "You want to come to Stacey's?" she asked.

Arnold pulled her to a quiet corner before answering. "Who's this Stacey chick? That kid from school? The snotty one?"

"Yeah," she said. "But you should come with."

Arnold shook his head. He laughed. "Yeah, me at Stacey's. Sure."

"Come on," she said.

"Hey," he said. He lifted her chin with his hand. "I'll see you later, okay?"

"Yeah?" she asked.

"Yeah, I'll hit you when this place closes. But I got to work still."

"Okay."

He rubbed his thumb on her cheek. He leaned closer and so did she, and this time, when he kissed her, he didn't just brush against her lips. He kissed her, and she kissed him back, tugging on his T-shirt to pull him closer.

"Later, okay?" he asked.

"Okay. You know where I live, right."

"Yeah, I do."

They said goodbye and she met her friends.

"Ready now?" asked Mish.

Leo laughed. There was nothing she'd wanted more than to go to Stacey's all night. She said yes.

TWENTY-TWO

Slideshow and Tears

October 19
The Present
11:00 P.M.

Dinner was over, the fat lady had sung. (The opera singer actually wasn't fat at all, but Ellie liked the expression.) Dessert had been served—a luscious buffet of delectable treats, not that anyone was partaking of any as this was mostly a fat-phobic Los Angeles–based crowd after all. But still, all that spun sugar was nice to look at.

The soprano was a hit; all the gays and a few of the grays were clustered around the singer, gushing and paying tribute. Ellie had hoped the famous diva would stay for a digestif and had hinted as much to the woman's manager, but apparently when you booked the famous, you booked only the performance; they were not behooved to actually socialize with you. She'd never seen anyone leave a party so fast—truly, it was impressive. A few arias and twenty thousand dollars later, the soprano was gone, trailing chiffon scarves in her wake.

Now everyone was invited to gather outside, in front of the

back wall, where the slideshow was about to start. The party planner was in an intense huddle with Ellie's assistant, both of them
working on the projector, hooking it up to the outdoor speakers. It
wasn't a difficult thing to do; she and Todd had always showed
movies in the back of the house when they had birthday parties for
the kids in LA, but they'd never done it in Palm Springs before,
and Nathaniel was having trouble getting the speakers to work.

Madison caught sight of Ellie and motioned her over. "Is Todd
ready?"

Todd was supposed to make a speech before the slideshow.
Everything had been planned to the second. But of course he was
nowhere to be found.

"I don't know where he is," she told them. "Can you get that
thing to work?"

Nathaniel frowned. "It should work. I plugged in the right
cable. I'm not really sure what's wrong."

"Where's Todd?" Madison asked again.

"I don't know!" said Ellie. "Just start without him! Forget the
speech!"

Todd was probably in some dark corner with that young piece
of tail he'd been flirting with earlier. Ellie thought of her friend
Jacklyn, who had slipped out of her wedding to screw the hot
bartender in the bathroom. No one had been the wiser, least of all
the groom, especially since the bride was back in time for the
toasts. It was the least Todd could do, Ellie thought, if he was doing the same. Finish fucking the bitch and get back in time to
toast your wife, goddammit.

Madison tapped her watch. "If we delay any longer, we'll be late for drag bingo," she said.

"I said get on with it," Ellie said, seething. "Nathaniel! Get that thing working already!"

"I'm trying," he said, furiously tapping the keyboard on his laptop.

The crowd was getting listless, and Ellie knew they would dissipate soon, wander off to separate corners to smoke cigarettes or gossip about her family. She wanted them all here. She had demanded a captive audience and her husband couldn't even do her the courtesy to show up for the speech he was supposed to give before the slideshow celebrating her life. She stabbed her fingernails into the palms of her hands.

"Nathaniel, I swear . . ." she began, just as the speakers overhead boomed to life with Green Day's "Time of Your Life."

Nathaniel gave her a thumbs-up. She looked around one last time for Todd. Where the hell was he?

Madison frantically gestured with the clicker.

Ellie threw up her hands. *Yes, I know. The drag queens. We'll be late for bingo. Fine.*

The slideshow started.

Click. HAPPY BIRTHDAY, ELLIE!

There was the photo of her and Todd when they were first dating, from the Emmys. He'd been so handsome, even with his bad frosted highlights. She still teased him about that, a straight man with highlights. He'd been so vain. And now he was probably fucking some twenty-year-old in the bathroom to make up for all the weight he'd gained. It was all an ego stroke, right? Pun definitely intended.

Another photo: of her and Sam, all of ten, the age Giggy was now. Sam had been such an awkward child. Oh, Sam. What had she confessed? That she was on probation, and there was something about not being able to come back in January? And there was more? WHAT? Did Todd know about this? He was supposed to deal with Samantha; that kid was part of his job. How could he let this happen? Ellie was trying to keep everything together and all Todd had to do was make sure everything in the family was fine, and he couldn't even do that.

Sam was mad at her and she wasn't anywhere in the crowd. Ellie couldn't find her. She wasn't watching the slideshow. Sam was mad because Ellie had to take a work call, and this wasn't the first time that had happened, but maybe the worst. Ellie sighed. Now, because her husband hadn't dealt with it, she would have to do it. She'd have to find Sam and figure out what was happening and, more important, why it happened in the first place. Ellie often felt pulled in so many different directions, and now look, she had taken her eye off the ball and Sam was flunking out of Stanford.

Ellie looked around. No Sam. No Todd. The busty girl was nowhere to be found either. Ellie's life was literally flashing before her eyes. Maybe this was what death was like, she thought and shuddered, remembering.

Where was *he*? Surely, he'd be at the party by now? What did he look like now? Why did he reach out now? What did he want?

He better not want money. She didn't have any. Oh my god, what if he wanted money?

She wrestled her thoughts away from the past.

More photos.

The family in Park City (the stupid house that cost too much money and was filled with ants). She would have to sell that house as soon as possible.

A sweet picture of Giggy.

Ellie loved her child with an ache. She knew she wasn't doing well at school, with all her issues, plus she was being bullied. The girls in her class were mean—why had Ellie even invited their parents? And some boy was hitting her, and they knew exactly who it was—the principal's kid. Todd said they had to go to the headmaster, not the principal, to deal with it. He was furious, and they'd have to figure out a strategy when they got back to Los Angeles.

Now there were photos from Wild & West shoots, as well as pictures of her company—the warehouses, all the employees waving. The company she had built from scratch, from sheer will. The company that might not exist by next week if she didn't get Mr. Harry Kim to put down his money to save them.

Her husband was having an affair, her stepdaughter was flunking out of college, her ten-year-old was being hazed, and the twins were out of control.

But hey, it all looked perfect on camera, didn't it? And wasn't that the point?

The lights came back on.

Ellie wiped her cheeks, and only then realized she'd been crying. She had a beautiful life. Why hadn't she appreciated it more? Why had she ever complained about it?

She loved it so much, but it was over, for so many reasons. Everything was over.

TWENTY-THREE

Truth or Dare

October 19
Twenty-Four Years Ago
11:00 P.M.

S tacey lived in one of the biggest houses Leo had ever seen. From afar, it looked almost like a castle, up on a hill, with a huge circular driveway. Leo had never been in this neighborhood before, and tried not to feel intimidated by the size and scale of the place. The house was surrounded by acres of trees, and she couldn't imagine what it was like, to have no neighbors on either side, to have all that space, all that land, to yourself and your family. Where she and Mish lived, people were crammed so tightly in a small space, there wasn't enough room for all of them, their pets, and all their junk. This is what it meant to be rich, to be wealthy, to have so much of everything, even air—it felt like there was more oxygen up here, like the air was cleaner (it was).

Brooks parked the car and they walked toward the house; they could hear the muffled sound of rap music coming from inside. Leo headed toward the front door, but Brooks shook his head.

"Party's out in the guesthouse. Stacey's not dumb enough to have everyone in their main house; her parents would freak."

He led them through the side gate, out toward the pool, which was covered for the season. The guesthouse was a smaller version of the main house, but its doors were open to the night, and its porch was filled with popular teens from their school, all the hot seniors, and even a few freshmen. Leo felt as if there was a spotlight on her as everyone craned to see who had arrived.

Mish seemed to know everyone, as she waved and said hello to several people standing in bunches, holding cans of beer, a few of the girls holding bottles of wine coolers. There was a Styrofoam ice chest full of drinks near the door, and Brooks added the remaining beers to the party haul. An entrance fee, or simply an offering to the party gods. A few more soccer players arrived and did the same thing.

Leo hung back, not quite sure where she fit in. She'd wanted so badly to be at this party and now she had no idea where to go. She didn't belong anywhere, and it would be weird to hang out with the kids from her class when they didn't hang out at school. She tried to appear nonchalant and casual, but it was hard when everyone was engaged in conversation, or laughing, or playing some kind of drinking game on the Ping-Pong table.

"You made it!"

Leo turned to see Shona Silverstein, grinning widely and holding out her arms for a hug.

"Oh hey!" said Leo.

"I thought you guys weren't going to stop by?" said Shona.

"Yeah, well, we changed our minds!" said Leo brightly. "Cool party."

"There she is!" said Mish, running over to give Shona a big bear hug from behind. "We're here!"

Shona laughed and almost spilled her drink. You'd think from the way she and Mish were acting they'd known each other forever.

"What's been up? What did you guys do tonight?" asked Shona.

"Not much. We hit the DQ, then Sparkle," said Mish, sounding a bit smug and as if they went to nightclubs any old day.

Shona was impressed. "You guys got in? Who was playing?"

Leo shrugged; she couldn't remember.

"Well, welcome, you guys haven't missed much," said Shona with a giggle.

"Should we say hi to Stacey?" Leo suggested.

Shona stared at her like it was the dumbest thing she'd ever heard. "Why?"

Leo colored. Her mom had brought her up to say hello to the host. She'd always drilled manners into her daughter's head. But it was clear she didn't know the first thing about high school parties.

"Half the people here don't even know whose party this is," said Mish.

"Pretty much," said Shona. "Besides, Stacey's passed out in the Jacuzzi upstairs. I'm supposed to make sure no one goes in the main house."

Mish went to see where Brooks had gone, and Leo followed

Shona into the guesthouse. Even in miniature, the place was bigger than her own house. It was two stories, with a full kitchen and dining room. In the living room, a few guys were playing video games on the television and Shona led Leo upstairs to the two bedrooms. A strong smell of pot wafted from the first closed door. "Drug room," explained Shona. "You want?" she asked, so casually that Leo understood there was no right or wrong answer to this question.

Leo shook her head.

"Let's see what's happening in here," her erstwhile host decided, knocking on the next bedroom door. "Hello!" said Shona.

They found a group of kids sitting in a circle with an empty wine cooler bottle in the middle, including Dave Griffin, from earlier at the mall. He looked up when they entered the room but didn't say hello.

"Oh my god, are you guys serious? What is this, middle school?" said Shona. "You're playing truth or dare?"

"Shut up, Shona!" yelled one of the girls.

A few of the boys laughed. "I don't remember Andie flashing her tits in middle school," said one of them.

"She didn't have tits in middle school, that's why," said Dave.

Andie, who was pulling her shirt down over her bra, stuck her tongue out at them. She crawled to the middle and spun the bottle.

It pointed at Leo.

"Truth or dare?" Andie demanded.

"Oh, I'm not playing," said Leo.

"Yeah, it's her birthday," said Shona. "Leave her alone."

"It's your birthday?"

"I thought it was Stacey's birthday?" someone said.

As if in answer, the door opened just then, and Mish and Brooks walked in. Mish was holding a plate of cupcakes, with a few candles stuck to the middle of one. Leo could see an *S* on another one. They were leftover birthday cupcakes from someone else's birthday, but on the other hand, they were the only birthday cupcakes she would get this evening.

"Happy birthday to you, happy birthday to you," Mish began to sing, and everyone else joined in.

She held the plate out and Leo leaned over.

"Wait!" said Mish. "You have to make a wish!"

Leo thought about it. Would she wish the night was over? Would she wish these were her friends? For another life? Other memories? She made her wish and blew out the candles.

Mish brought out her camera again and asked Shona to take a photo of the three of them. Leo held up her cupcake, Brooks and Mish on either side of her.

"There you go," said Shona, handing Mish back her camera and handing Leo the photo. "Cute."

Leo waved it a few times, watching as the picture slowly developed. There they were, the three of them. She grimaced. Was that what she really looked like? She should brush her hair, and she'd thought she looked so cute at the beginning of the night, but now she just looked tired.

"Ew, I look awful," she said.

Brooks took it from her hand. "I think we look great," he said, and put it in his pocket.

"Um, what if she wanted that?" Mish scolded.

"You want it?"

"No, you can keep it," Leo told him. She liked that he wanted to have a picture of her, something to remember her by.

TWENTY-FOUR

Four and Twenty

October 19
The Present
11:00 P.M.

Even if pot was sort of legal in Los Angeles now—and it would be a few years until it was *fully* legal—at this moment in time, you still needed a doctor's prescription to get ahold of it. And they couldn't prescribe it for anxiety or stress or any psychological issue either—Todd learned that the hard way. You had to say you had back pain, or some kind of chronic physical condition. Todd wished he'd been able to get some for his dad, who'd died of cancer a few years back. Dad had said he wanted to try it, because he never had, and he was curious especially now that he had cancer and was dying.

Todd had offered to get some for him, but his mom had said no. His mother, who even at the end of his father's life, forbade her husband from having any sort of fun. They were happily married for fifty years, strict Catholics, and his mother was horrified to think her husband would turn into a pothead right before the end. She'd shaken her head firmly no, and that had settled it. Dad meekly complied as he always did. Perhaps that's what a happy marriage was about, subsuming your own desires for the happiness of your spouse. Even, you know, on your deathbed.

Dad died before ever taking a toke.

Not Todd, though.

But yeah, even if pot was sort of legal, Todd still found he needed to hide from his guests when he took a hit. He had a legal license and everything, procured from a seedy "doctor" whose office was conveniently down the street from the Ventura Boulevard pot emporiums. The Valley was riddled with pot joints; you couldn't turn a corner without running into one: the Weed, Buds & Roses, 420 Docs, the Stash, the Collective, WHTC, Urban Treez. Todd passed them every day when he dropped off the twins at Glenwood Prep. No wonder even the headmaster's kid was caught dealing; pot was everywhere.

Supposedly, there were Hollywood parties where they passed around trays of joints and lines of coke like they were candy, but again, he'd never been to one. Maybe he didn't have the right friends; maybe because he'd been the boss for all those years, people didn't invite him to those kinds of events. At every party he went to, people still hid in the bathrooms or in the bushes to do their drugs. It was only polite after all.

Right now he was standing in the alley behind his house, behind the hedges, and he brought out the joint he'd rolled earlier. When Sam was twelve, he'd thrown out all the drugs in his house—the Adderall, the Ritalin, the vials of coke, the dime bags of pot. He didn't want her snooping around and finding it. It was bad enough that her mother didn't hide her addictions. Montserrat was the worst about that sort of thing—one of her boyfriends (the one after the real estate guy, the plastic surgeon) died of a heroin overdose. Todd wanted Sam to know at least one parent who didn't partake. So for years while Sam was in middle school and high school, he'd stopped doing drugs. Ellie wasn't a big druggie anyway—she was a model and wasn't averse to doing a line here or there or eating a pot gummy once in a while. But she mainlined her career. That's what got her high.

It was like that when he'd run the network too; he wasn't a partyer. He didn't go to nightclubs; he used it to stay up at work, to get everything done. Okay, sometimes he did it for fun, but mostly it was to stay up late in the editing room or to read scripts, but that all ended once Sam was old enough to notice.

Now he just smoked pot. Once in a while. At parties, in the bushes. He lit the joint and took a long drag. He'd have to give a speech before the slideshow soon.

He needed to calm his nerves.

Sure, he could give a speech. For the longest time, that was the biggest part of his job, giving speeches about their programming slate. Also part of his job was congratulating everyone. He was good at it. Everyone said Todd made them feel appreciated. The biggest showrunners wanted to work for him because he made them all feel loved. It was silly what people wanted, how a little gratitude went a long way. If people asked, Todd would say almost ninety percent of his success came from being able to communicate well. Except why couldn't he talk to his wife? Why couldn't he tell her?

Ellie was the love of his life, his one true love, but she wasn't even his second wife. She was his fourth. She'd laughed when she found out. "Wife number four; are you fucking kidding me, Todd? You're only thirty-five!" she'd cackled.

How had he married so many people in so short a time? Well, his first wife, Amy, was his high school sweetheart. They'd eloped after graduation, to Atlantic City. It was a mistake. He was going to Harvard, he was ruining his entire future. He reneged on the deal. They never filed the marriage certificate, so in a way, they'd never been married. Wife number two was his college sweetheart. He had a pattern. Once again, married right after graduation and divorced while he was still in business school. She'd cheated on him with his best friend, Dan. Goodbye, Heather. Heather was one of those formidable mommy moguls now. She'd started some new media company for moms by moms. She and Dan dated for a while but broke up a few months later. She was married to some top music exec; when Todd was at the network, he'd run into him once in a while. The guy didn't seem to know Todd had once been married to his wife.

Wife number three was Montserrat, and everyone knew that story. But as he liked to tell Ellie, he'd gotten it right on the fourth try. Ellie was the only one for him. He only wished they'd met sooner. And even in his earlier, unhappier relationships, he'd been faithful. He'd never cheated on any of his wives. Never. He was—what did they call it—a serial monogamist.

But Ellie, Ellie had a wild past. He figured as much when he'd taken her to the Oscars one year and they'd bumped into one of those actors every girl had a crush on in high school. That guy. He couldn't remember his name, but the guy had leered at Ellie and said, "Oh, we've met," in this meaningful way. Todd knew that meant the guy had jumped her bones. Later, when he asked her about it, Ellie had laughed and told him yeah, she'd slept with him all right; she could never forget because he had the smallest wiener she'd ever seen. It made him feel better, sort of.

At least that strange dude at the party turned out to be a process server—for their dog, of all things! But still, it didn't explain the texts on her phone. Those texts on the phone . . . That was a bummer. And he was supposed to make a speech? About how much he loved her? When she was cheating on him with someone?

I need you.

Don't leave me.

Had she ever texted Todd those words?

There was a rustling noise as someone came through the hedges and into his hiding place. Todd tensed.

"Hey, man, what's up?"

Todd looked up apprehensively, but relaxed into a smile. He clapped the guy on the back. "Hey, Sanjay."

He liked Sanjay. Sanjay was his friend too. Maybe the guy had started out as Archer's connection and was one of Ellie's best friends, but he and Sanjay were buds. He passed the joint over.

"Thanks," Sanjay said, taking a long puff. "So what's going on?"

"Not much," said Todd. "That's the problem."

"Are you looking?" asked Sanjay.

Todd shrugged. "No one wants an old media dude to run their new media companies."

Sanjay made a sympathetic grunt.

"It's fine, I'll figure something out. Maybe go back to producing," he said. Maybe, there was always a maybe. Maybe he could even go back to what he learned in college. Architecture. Why not?

"If you ever need anything . . ." said Sanjay, passing the joint back.

Todd nodded. "Thanks, man."

"Everything all right?"

"Other than the fact that we're almost bankrupt?"

"No!"

Todd shrugged. "It'll be all right."

"Are you sure?"

"Yeah." He shrugged. One way or another, they'd be all right. Maybe they wouldn't be able to live like this anymore, maybe they'd lose all their friends; no one liked poor. Poor *smelled*. Poor was catching. This crowd tolerated his failure only because his wife was such a success. But once they found out Ellie's company was floundering? That she and Todd couldn't be counted on to buy that ten-thousand-dollar table at the gala or jet down to Cabo at a moment's notice? Who'd hang out with them then?

He'd made the mistake of thinking all those people he worked with—all those fancy producers with their bungalows on the lot and those famous actors who always took him to Lakers games and those hot actresses who laughed at all his jokes—were his friends. Maybe some of them were; a few of them were here tonight—guys from HBS who ran the big agencies now, his old mentor at the network, but no one else. Those other people who'd kissed his ass all those years were never his friends; they were his subjects, and the king was dead.

Sanjay had a quizzical look on his face. "What's going on with Ellie's company? I thought she found a partner?"

"Did she? Beats me. She never tells me anything," said Todd.

"Hmmm," said Sanjay, who was too polite to comment.

Todd flicked the last of the joint into the grass and stubbed it out. "Come on, I've got to make a speech. Pretty sure my wife is freaking out by now."

TWENTY-FIVE

Dare

October 19
Twenty-Four Years Ago
11:15 P.M.

They ended up playing truth or dare, because it turned out that no one could say no to Shona. Leo sat cross-legged against the wall. So far, the bottle had eluded her, and she had watched in amusement as a few of the boys failed at some party tricks, and a few of the girls flashed their bras or had to pull their underwear up from their jeans to show them what they were wearing.

The bottle landed on Scott, one of the lacrosse players on Brooks's team. "Truth or dare," said Andie, the bossy senior who seemed to run the game.

"Truth," said Scott.

"Who do you think is prettier, Leo or Mish?" asked Andie.

The crowd hooted. Pitting two girls against each other was a favorite question. So far, they'd done Megan versus Shona (Megan), Andie versus Lila (Lila), and now Leo versus Mish.

"You don't have to answer that," said Leo, shaking her head.

"Oh, but that one's easy. Leo," said Scott with a grin.

"Fuck you, Scott!" said Mish from the back, where she was cuddled with Brooks.

Leo laughed, trying not to feel too pleased, too smug. The bottle spun again, and the next few people chose dares, which were pretty mild. Dave Griffin had to sniff everyone's armpits, Olivia Chang had to do four cartwheels in a row, then Deacon Walker had to switch clothes with Avery O'Rourke, which took a while since they had to trade turns in the bathroom to do it.

While they were waiting, the seniors started talking about—what else—college.

"So are you doing Early Decision or Early Action at Brown?" Shona asked Dave.

"Probably Early Action; I don't want to be tied down too much. What if I get into Harvard?" he said.

"My mom is going to kill me if I don't get into Yale," said Olivia, who was probably going to be valedictorian.

"Same," lamented Andie. "What about you, Brooks?"

"U of Michigan is my top choice; my dad went there. Notre Dame is my safety," he said.

"What about you guys?" Shona asked, turning to Mish and Leo. "I mean, I know you guys are sophomores, so you have some time."

Mish snort-laughed and didn't answer. Leo hid her face behind her hair and took another sip of her beer. "I don't know, maybe just Lake."

"The community college?" gagged Andie, overhearing their conversation.

"Harvard on the Hill," smirked Dave.

Shona slapped him on the arm. "RUDE! What's wrong with Lake?"

"Nothing but everything," joked Deacon, returning from the bathroom, wearing Avery's tube top.

"Lake! Ew!" laughed Avery, who was swimming in Deacon's striped rugby jersey.

Leo cringed, and Mish met her eyes. Leo understood now, how hard it was for Mish to hang out with Brooks's crowd.

The bottle spun again. This time, the dares were less innocent. The boys began to demand time in the bathroom. The girls shrieked and protested, but they went into the bathroom with the boys anyway.

Leo, who was still smarting from the embarrassment of the Lake College situation, wasn't paying attention when the bottle landed on her.

It was Dave's turn. But before she could choose truth or dare, he didn't give her a choice. "I dare you to kiss me in the bathroom. Come on."

"Leo—no!" said Mish. "Leave her alone, Dave! Leo, you don't have to!"

But everyone had done it. Andie had gone in with Deacon. Shona with Scott. Why should she be any different?

Dave looked her over coolly. Leo didn't like the way he was looking at her, but she ignored it. He'd ignored her at the mall and all night, but now she had his attention. Plus, she was just trying to fit in. It was only a few minutes alone in the bathroom. What were they, in middle school? She could handle him.

She stood up and followed him into the bathroom.

Dave locked the door behind him.

He turned the lights off.

Leo braced herself for a kiss. She'd already kissed one boy to-night, what was another?

But before she knew what was happening, he'd pushed her down on her knees and unzipped his fly. His hand was on her head, insistent.

What was going on, what was happening? This wasn't what she'd agreed to, and her heart was pounding. She was woozy, and a little scared.

Why had she volunteered to do this? How did she get here? On her knees in Stacey Anders's guest bathroom with some jock asshole's hand on her head?

She scrambled, but Dave held her there, in front of his crotch. There was an edge to his voice, a menace she hadn't noticed before.

"Come on, kiss me."

She did.

TWENTY-SIX

Brandy and Cigars

(or Cigarettes and Chocolate Milk)

October 19
The Present
11:30 P.M.

"Where were you?" Ellie demanded when she finally caught sight of Todd. He had emerged from the bushes. Was that where he was fucking that girl? The bushes? What was this, Central Park? But he was walking over with Sanjay, who'd come from the hedges too, and Todd's pants didn't have telltale marks on the knees. So maybe Todd *wasn't* fucking that girl in the hedges? Ellie was confused. What was he doing over there, then?

"Sorry, babe," he said. Todd smelled like weed. Cannabis. You were supposed to say *cannabis* now and not *weed*. Weed was trashy. Weed was Jeff Bridges as The Dude heading off to the bowling alley. Weed was Beavis and Butthead. Cannabis was Silicon Valley. Cannabis was Coachella, but the VIP room.

The caterers were passing trays of Calvadoses and Cubans. The apple brandy served in snifters and the cigars hand-rolled on the premises by a company her party planner hired for the evening. The sweet smell of tobacco and brandy infused the night.

"We did the slideshow already," Madison accused as Nathaniel hit the lights back on.

"Okay, okay, but I can still make a speech, right?" he asked.

Madison rolled her eyes.

Ellie sighed. "Sure. Why not."

He kissed her forehead. "Calm down, babe."

Todd stepped up to the microphone. "Hello, hello, how is everyone? As most of you know, and I hope you do, I'm Todd, Ellie's husband. Your host. First of all, we'd like to thank everyone here tonight, especially those who traveled from so far away to be here today, and that includes our friends from the Valley." (Polite laughter from the crowd, since technically the Valley was part of Los Angeles, but it was far away *spiritually* and stylistically, even though half of the people at the party actually lived there. The Valley was to LA what New Jersey was to New York.) "Tonight means so much to us; we are so happy to have everyone here to share such a meaningful moment in our lives." He coughed.

"I just wanted to say a few words about this beautiful woman whom I'm proud to call my wife." He turned to Ellie directly. She really was so beautiful, even though she was older now, ten years older than when they'd first met, and starting to have those little lines on the side of her eyes, which only made her more beautiful. He hated that frozen Botox look. He was glad Ellie did it sparingly, or had a really good doctor. "Ellie, you are the bravest, smartest, most hardworking woman I know. I am floored every day by your energy, your enthusiasm, your whole-hearted dedication to our life and our children. I am so incredibly lucky. Nothing would be possible without you. You make everything happen. The best day of my life was the day that we met."

Awwwww from the crowd.

"You don't look a day over thirty-nine!"

Everyone laughed.

"I wish you the happiest birthday, and here's to many, many more." He raised his champagne glass—(thanks, Madison, for putting one in hand right on time)—and the crowd did the same. "To Ellie!"

"To Ellie!" they chorused.

Clink, clink, clink.

Ellie blushed. It was exactly the kind of speech she wanted her husband to give, and yet she couldn't enjoy it. She wasn't even listening. She hardly heard a word he'd said. Her mind was whirling with doubt. Why had he looked so relieved when the process server handed her the papers for the lawsuit? What did he know? And who was that girl he was talking to earlier?

But before she could dwell on it too much, Sanjay was already elbowing Todd out of the way. "Ellie didn't ask me to make a speech tonight, but I wanted to anyway," he said, his brown face crinkling in a smile.

"I didn't ask anyone to make one!" she yelled. (Except Todd of course.) She'd only wanted a speech from her husband. Even if she didn't actually listen to it.

She didn't need speeches, didn't need toasts; she didn't need anyone to throw bouquets at her feet, didn't need it and didn't want it. But perhaps it was too much to expect that anyone would not thank her for this weekend, for this party. They were her friends, after all. She had to remember that.

So one by one, they stood up and paid their tribute. First Sanjay with the usual story of how they met (*She called me the Math Nerd!*) and some fun memories of their kids growing up together, how they'd flipped that Jet Ski in Belize. (He was good enough not to mention all that trouble with Archer in Dubai.)

The speeches kept coming. A few of her girlfriends, the former models, with way too many anecdotes of fashion-show backstage high jinks and partying at clubs *and remember when we were almost kidnapped in Dubai by that crazy sheik!* (Which we would sooner forget; thanks for bringing it up.) Then the fellow parents from the kids' schools, generic, bland speeches about how lucky they were to know her and Todd (they were right about that). It was sad to realize no one truly knew her. No one from her past, no one who knew her from before. No family either. Her mom had passed a few years ago, and as for her dad, he was, as they say, better off dead.

The only one at the party who knew her as a teen was Archer, and he'd been interested only in her body and her youth then. He didn't even know anything about where she'd come from. Of course, Mishon had been invited, but she'd sent last-minute regrets. Maybe she couldn't stand to see Ellie this way, even if Ellie had been Ellie for so long now. But maybe she couldn't stomach whom Ellie had become for one more night.

———

"Did you know Samantha is flunking out of college?" Ellie asked when the speeches were over and she found her husband in the corner, eating a second piece of Milk Bar Crack Pie. "Really, Todd? Another piece?"

He crammed the last bite into his mouth and shot her a look of contempt. "No one else is eating. It's all going to waste."

"Yeah, your waist," she said.

"Stop being a bully."

"Okay, right, I'm sorry," she said, shoulders slumping. "Did you know?"

"About Sam?" He frowned. "I think so. Some kind of problem with plagiarism?"

"What? She didn't mention that, only that she had to pull up her grades. Todd! You were supposed to be on top of that!"

"I know, I know, I'm sorry. I thought she mentioned something, but I figured she'd deal with it. She's always been able to before." He had crumbs around his mouth and she wished he would wipe them off; he looked like a pig. Honestly, what was she so worried about? What twenty-year-old would want to sleep with him?

"Well, she's not!" Samantha wasn't dealing with it, and neither was Todd. No one was dealing with it, which meant that, as usual, she would have to fix this. What was new? It was so tiring always being the one who did everything. *Often. Often* the one who did everything. Fuck, what difference did it make? Always, often, it came down to the same thing, didn't it? Just another chore on her list. "Sam is not dealing with it, Todd! She's going to get kicked out! Of Stanford!" *The absolute horror.*

How would she face her friends? What would everyone say? It was too humiliating. She had enjoyed Sam's academic triumph so much as if it were hers. While her friends told stories of kids slinking home freshman year, not able to hack it, or having to send them to community college, of all places, after paying hundreds of thousands of dollars on private school tuition, Ellie had been smug with the knowledge that Sam was securely perched at the top of the collegiate heap. So this was what it meant when they said pride cometh before a fall.

"Stanford, Todd! Stanford!" She didn't have to say any more than that; he, of all people, understood.

"Crap," he said.

"That's all you can say about it? Crap?"

"What else is there to say?"

Ellie wanted to strangle him. He'd gone to Harvard, graduated cum laude, of course, although he explained later that *everyone* graduated Harvard with honors—that it was actually difficult *not to.* Still, it seemed so easy for him—Harvard, then Harvard Business School (H!B!S!), his luxe little life. So what if Sam had flunked out since there was supposed to be a trust fund somewhere, right? Except she'd emptied the kids' trusts to keep the business afloat too. (Shhhhh.) There were no trust funds, not anymore. At least the kids still had their college funds. For now.

Ellie had wanted to go to college but never had the chance, never had the grades. She'd always wanted to be one of those girls who went away, to one of those fancy East Coast schools. But girls like her didn't go to college; at the very most they went to community college, aka thirteenth grade. Girls like her weren't supposed to end up at this house, with these friends, at this party, and yet here she was, against all those odds. She'd made it. She was the American Dream.

"Of course you don't care," she accused.

"I care!" He took another slice of pie. The man had no self-discipline. It was pathetic.

She'd had enough. She was going to confront him. "And by the way, who's that floozy you've been talking to all night?"

"What floozy?"

"The one with the boobs!" She gestured toward her chest and mimed making mounds out of them. Not that she hadn't had a little work done herself, but then, who didn't? Just a little lift every couple of years; when they began to sag, she went right back to get them hauled up again. It was like getting a new handbag, and cost about as much. Except she had to hole up in a hotel suite for a few days, but Todd was pretty good about it. He always drained her bandages for her. Whatever. "The little slut you've been hanging around all night!"

Todd put down his plate and fork. "I don't know what the hell you're talking about!"

"Oh, really." Her tone suggested she didn't believe him one bit.

"Yeah."

"Ellie, I am not having an affair."

"Prove it!"

He waved his hands in the air in frustration. "How?"

"I don't know!" She looked over her shoulder. Guests were starting to stare their way. It would be just the icing on the cake for everyone to see her marriage melt down right at the height of her party.

He pointed his beer bottle at her. "What about you?"

"What *about* me?"

"I saw the texts on your phone."

"Oh, *that*," she said. He'd seen? He saw the texts? Shit! She tried to arrange her face into an innocent expression.

Todd leaned over so that his face was inches from hers. "Yeah, *that*."

"It's nothing," she said dismissively. So what if he'd seen the texts. They didn't give away anything. There was nothing there to feel the least bit guilty about.

"Really?"

She raised her chin. "Yeah, you'll meet him later. He's no one. It's nothing. Just someone I used to know."

"Why don't I believe you?"

"Well, you should, because it's nothing."

"So where is he, then?"

"I don't know. Maybe he's not showing up."

"Are you sad about that?"

"Not really, why?"

"It didn't seem that way on your phone."

"Wait, what?" She was confused now, and starting to think that maybe Todd was thinking of something else. "You know, honey, I'm not even sure we're talking about the same thing now."

"Um, Ellie?" said Madison-and-Lex, coming up to them with an anxious look on her face.

"WHAT!" Ellie whirled around, murderous.

"The photographer from *Vanity Fair* is here."

TWENTY-SEVEN

Double Dare

October 19
Twenty-Four Years Ago
11:30 P.M.

Leo was still wiping her mouth when she came back to the room. David swaggered back with a shit-eating grin.

"You okay?" asked Mish. She looked at David suspiciously.

"Yeah, I'm fine." It was just like that afternoon, Leo thought. Did she have a sign on her head that said she would do these kinds of things to guys? And it wasn't as if that had been the only time either. Maybe she was just that kind of girl.

"I told you not to go in there with him," said Mish accusingly, like it was Leo's fault. Maybe it was.

I didn't know that was going to happen. I didn't know. I thought he just wanted a kiss. I thought that was all he wanted.

"I told you, I'm fine!" she snapped. Could Mish just stop looking at her like that?

The game resumed, but somehow the bathroom dares were over. Leo wondered if Andie and Shona had to do what she'd done, but if they had, they weren't showing it. Shona was sitting on Deacon's lap, like they were best buds, and Andie was opening another beer. David excused himself and went to see what the other jock assholes were doing in the other rooms.

Leo hugged her knees to her chest. The bottle fell on Brooks next. Andie couldn't wait to pounce. "Leo or Mish?" she asked with an evil glint in her eyes.

"Um, one of them's his girlfriend? No fair!" hollered Deacon.

Andie snapped, "Yeah, but the game is called truth!"

Leo's cheeks were burning. Her feelings were in turmoil; she wasn't sure exactly what had just happened with David, and how she had gotten there, but she knew she blamed Mish.

"What do you mean, he might like her over his girlfriend?" asked Deacon.

"It could happen!" Andie argued.

Brooks smiled. "Sorry, Leo. I choose Mish, of course."

"Boring!" said Andie.

The game went on, and a few moved away from the circle and started playing a drinking game instead. They were low on snacks and drinks, so Mish offered to replenish the stash and grab some beer from the cooler.

"And maybe some chips or crackers?" Leo asked Mish. She was fully sober now. The taste of David's sour penis in her mouth had woken her up. She couldn't pretend that hadn't happened, but she badly wanted to forget as soon as possible. Maybe if she put something else in her mouth, she would lose the taste.

The bottle landed on Brooks again. He was leaning back, knees crossed in front of him, casual and languid. "Dare," he said, obviously bored.

"Kiss Leo," said Olivia.

He raised an eyebrow. Mish still hadn't returned.

The girls began to titter. "Come on!" said Andie. "It's a game!"

"Yeah and you already kissed Dave," sneered Olivia.

Leo colored hotly. Whatever she had done back there, that wasn't a kiss.

David had pressed himself against her lips, forced her mouth open, and then he was inside her, while he held the back of her head, his hands heavy and strong so that she couldn't move, she couldn't breathe, and he'd moved her head back and forth, then slammed himself all the way back into her throat, oh god, it was disgusting, and she was just trying to breathe, and then he'd . . .

She closed her eyes, willing the memory away.

When she opened them, Brooks was already moving toward her. She froze.

"Is this okay?" he whispered.

"Yeah." She shrugged. She didn't care. Whatever. Like Andie said, it was a game.

His lips were wet and soft and the kiss was sweeter than the wine cooler she'd been drinking. He put a gentle hand against her cheek. It was so sweet she felt tears come to her eyes. It was everything she'd hoped for. Unexpected. Like a present. Like a birthday surprise.

This was nice. This wasn't like the other thing. (Thank god no one knew about the other thing.)

Her eyes were still closed and her tongue was still in his mouth when she heard a distinctive voice cut through the silence.

"Um." It was Mish. She was back.

TWENTY-EIGHT

Vanities

October 19
The Present
11:35 P.M.

So the *Vanity Fair* photographer finally arrived when the party was almost winding down? It was practically midnight! They would be heading out to the first after-party soon—the drag queens and their raucous game of bingo. Ellie tamped down her irritation, as it would lead to frown lines and wrinkles in the subsequent photographs and there were some things even injectables couldn't hide.

"Hi, I'm Ellie Stinson," she said, dropping the "de Florent" because Todd was standing right next to her. "Welcome to our home," she said, the consummate hostess.

"You're the birthday girl?"

"That's me!"

The photographer was a rumpled, distracted older gentleman in a safari vest. Ellie knew the type; she had worked with many a lensman during her short-lived modeling career. There was the lecher who'd gotten into the business to ogle pretty girls and ask them to take off their clothes (most of whom would later be fired during the industry's MeToo movement); then there was the artist type who was annoyed he'd never made it in the galleries and was stuck shooting stupid bitches in clothes; and there was the celebrity stalker, who was in it for the proximity to boldfaced names (most of those started out as paparazzi); and the actual photojournalists, guys who had gone to war zones and shot famine and violence but had gotten too old, or were close to retirement, and so ended up doing party photographs for the newswires and the photo agencies and the occasional glossy magazine.

This was one of them.

"Can I just have a moment to touch up my makeup?" she asked. "Do you want to take a few shots of the atmosphere? And Madison here can get you a guest list if you want to shoot some people now."

The photographer—let's call him Gary since Ellie couldn't be bothered to find out his name—removed a crumpled piece of paper from his vest. "Um, I think this is for Vanities, so really I don't need that many pictures."

"Vanities? I thought this was for a four-page profile. Madison!"

"Yes?"

"I thought this was a profile. Isn't someone going to interview me later?"

"Um, they haven't decided yet."

"PARDON?" asked Ellie, who had learned to use that word only after hanging out with Blake, who visibly shuddered every time she asked, "What?"

"They changed editors. They fired the one who ordered the

profile, and the new editor doesn't know what she wants to do yet," Madison explained.

Ellie seethed. All this expense and effort and all she would show for it was one dinky photo in the collage of photos in the middle of the magazine that no one looked at? If she was even that lucky! Okay, fine, but maybe there was still a chance she could get a profile? At the very least, she would settle for being the featured celebrity in My Stuff, which was at least a half page and she could plug her line, since Wild & West was certainly her stuff.

"Shall we get a family shot?" asked Gary.

"Yes, let's," Ellie agreed.

The kids were wrangled, and Todd had managed to locate Samantha, who, curiously enough, was talking to the girl Todd had been speaking to earlier. Ellie fumed at the audacity of her husband—flaunting his little minx in front of the children! She made a face, and the camera flashed. She would look constipated in the shots, which wouldn't end up in *Vanity Fair* at all but in some obscure bottom-feeding blog that no one had heard of and would turn out to be run by some twelve-year-old in Idaho.

When the photo shoot was done, Ellie immediately turned to her husband. "You're fucking her, aren't you?"

"Who?"

"Her!" she whispered fiercely, gesturing to the hot young thing.

"Her!" yelped Todd. "I thought you said you'd talked to Sam!"

"I did! What does Sam have to do with it?" asked Ellie as Sam walked over, hand in hand with the buxom blonde. "Mom," she said. "I want you to meet Sofia."

"Oh, hi," said Ellie, trying not to sound too shrill.

"Hi, Mrs. Stinson. Sam told me so much about you."

"I wish I could say the same."

Sam colored. "We're dating."

"Oh!" Ellie said. So she had been right. Her little stepdaughter *was* a cute little butch lesbian. "Oh! Which means . . ."

Todd glared at her.

Ellie laughed, somewhat hysterically.

"Sof, why don't you go grab a drink. I need to talk to my mom and dad," said Sam.

TWENTY-NINE

Truth

October 19
Twenty-Four Years Ago
11:35 P.M.

Leo thought Mish would be mad for sure. For a while she just stood there, watching her boyfriend and her best friend disentangle themselves from each other. But instead of getting mad, she walked up to them and said, "No fair; I can do that too." Then she turned to Leo and kissed her on the lips.

Leo was startled, but she opened her mouth, and they kissed, slowly and deeply.

A few of the boys in the room began to clap.

Brooks cleared his throat and put a hand on each of their shoulders. "All right, all right, you've made your point."

Mish grinned as she stepped away, and winked at Leo.

Leo felt her knees wobble. It was surreal, to be kissing one and then the other. She couldn't decide who was a better kisser. "Um, where's another bathroom?" she asked Shona. She just needed to be alone right then.

But both bathrooms in the guesthouse were taken, so Leo

asked if she could go to the main house. Shona didn't seem to hear her and Leo suddenly didn't care if there was a no-kids-in-the-main-house rule. She just needed to get away from that room, which was claustrophobic all of a sudden.

The game was effectively over, and now people were just making out in corners, not even caring who could see. Mish had pulled Brooks to one and was straddling his lap, grinding on him, while he had fisted his hands in her long hair. Leo wasn't sure she wanted to be there to see what happened next.

Leo made her way out and opened the sliding door to the main house. There were a few kids hanging out in the kitchen, but no one even looked up when she entered or seemed to care that she was there. She debated asking them where the bathroom was, but decided that would bring too much attention to her presence, and it probably wasn't too hard to find one anyway; this place probably had like eight or ten bathrooms.

She walked tentatively down the hallway, opening doors. She found the coat closet, a linen closet, a closet that seemed to hold only cleaning supplies, and a room where a lazy white cat hissed at her when she opened it.

"Oh god, is everyone still here? Why are there people in the main house?" asked Stacey, who walked out of one of the back bedrooms, yawning.

"Um, I think so," said Leo. "Hi, Stacey."

Stacey crinkled her eyes at Leo, trying to place her. "You're . . . Brooks's friend, right?"

"Yes."

"Cool."

"Thanks for having me," said Leo, like her mom had taught her.

Stacey waved dismissively, as if she didn't care either way. Stacey didn't seem bothered that she was there, and Leo felt more confident as she continued to navigate the hallways, supposedly looking for a bathroom when in reality she was now giving herself a tour. It was a lot bigger than Brooks's house. Bigger bedrooms with wall-to-wall carpeting in each bedroom. There were four or five bedrooms; she lost count. Stacey's older sisters were already in college or graduated. Like Stacey, they had been the legendary queens of their grade; everyone was obsessed with the Anders girls. Their rooms were shrines to their childhood, pristine and untouched. Stacey's room was plush, all white and gold with splashes of pink and green; she had a four-poster princess bed, with a built-in desk and neat shelves full of books and knick-knacks. There was a poster board filled with pictures of Stacey with her friends, Stacey with her family, Stacey at camp, Stacey in Paris, Stacey at the winter formal, the junior prom, the senior fling, too many pictures to mention.

Nothing terrible happens in a room like this, thought Leo. No one yells at you, no one surprises you in the middle of the night. No one creeps into your bedroom without warning. No one forces you to give them a blow job in the bathroom. Did that even happen? It was like a bad dream.

She picked up one of the oversize teddy bears on Stacey's bed, when the door opened. She jumped as if she'd been caught stealing. She placed the bear back on the cashmere throw.

"There you are. What a place, right?" said Mish. Her hair was messy and her clothes were askew, as if she'd gotten dressed in a hurry. Leo wondered if they'd made use of one of the two lock-able bedrooms in the guesthouse.

"Yeah," said Leo. She knew Mish was thinking the same thing she was, comparing their messy, squalid, sad little bedrooms to this serene abode.

They looked at Stacey's pictures for a while.

Brooks found them a few minutes later. "Ready to go?" he asked, swinging his keys.

The ride back was silent, and not a good silent, not the friendly silence that Leo and Mish had shared on the bus. Leo and Mish. Mish and Leo. They were one and the same, they were sisters from another mother. That's what they always said. More than blood, more than family, they had each other. Whatever was happening between them now was stupid. It was a cliché. It wasn't even about Brooks.

Because as the minutes ticked by, it was clear that Mish was pissed. Leo knew she was mad because when Mish was mad, she got quiet.

"Is this the right street?" asked Brooks, peering at the metal wire fence at the entrance to the neighborhood.

"You can just let us off here," said Mish, unfastening her seat belt.

"No, I said I'd drive you guys." Brooks was abashed; it was apparent he felt guilty about what had happened earlier and wanted to make it up to Mish.

She sighed and gave him directions so that he drove up to the two little houses on the back lot, tiny little trailers on cinder blocks. Why did they call them trailers? They looked just like houses, like anyone's house, with a door and windows. These were just smaller and dingier and crappier. None of the lights were on in either of their houses as none of their parents were ever home.

"Well, this is us," said Mish, sounding defensive.

"Okay," said Brooks. "It's nice."

Mish rolled her eyes. "Of course it isn't."

"Babe, you know I don't care where you live."

"I care," said Mish, an edge to her voice. "Well, now you know."

"It's fine; I don't know what you're so worried about."

"Let's not talk about it right now," said Mish, eyeing Leo in the back seat.

Leo tried to make herself smaller as she unlocked the car door. "Thanks for the ride," she said. She didn't wait to say any more goodbyes. She just wanted to be home, finally.

THIRTY

Truth?

The first time she had met Samantha, the little girl hardly said a word. Ellie worried she was mute at first, but Todd hadn't mentioned anything about that, so she was probably just shy. Ellie didn't know a lot of kids, other than her own baby. She thought most of them were kind of annoying, actually. She'd hated babysitting when she was a teenager. She was tired, Giggy still wasn't sleeping through the night, and now she had a new boyfriend, which meant between being up for her kid and being kept up all night by her new man, Ellie was exhausted. She didn't have time to try and make friends with this skinny little kid who looked at her with her big brown eyes like Ellie was some kind of monster.

Stepmonster.

The kind that steals daddies away.

The little girl probably hated her guts.

Except it wasn't like that. Turned out Sam was just shy. She was worried that Ellie wouldn't want her, that Ellie would take

her away from her dad, the only stable presence in her life, that
Ellie's presence meant Sam would have to live with her mom all
the time. No one wanted that, least of all Montserrat, who had
already dumped the real estate guy and moved on to a plastic
surgeon for the discount.

"Hey," Ellie had said. "Are you Sam?"

Sam nodded.

"I'm Ellie. I'm your dad's friend. I'm going to be your friend
too, okay?"

If Ellie had known then what she knew now, would she have
fought so hard? Because once Montserrat dumped the doctor and
decided that she wanted her hot young ex-husband back, only to
discover Todd had moved on, she had unleashed the hounds, so
to speak. She'd dragged them through seven circles of hell to keep
them from her kid. In return, Todd and Ellie had fought as hard
as they could. They used Ellie's money like a cudgel, paid as many
lawyers and private investigators and counselors as they needed to
try and keep Montserrat away from Sam. It was the judgment of
Solomon, except the only thing being torn apart were their bank
accounts. Ellie lost a small fortune on this kid. A year's profits
from the fall collection. Sometimes, she told her girlfriends, she
would never have married Todd if she knew he came with so
much baggage. (Except she *did* know, didn't she? She knew that
she was wife number four, she knew he was a little out of his
mind, the way he collected wives like Patek watches.)

She liked to fantasize about an alternate past, one without

Todd. She would have been fine, a single mom to Giggy, co-parenting with Archer across the pond. She would have continued dating people on television, or the boyfriend right before she went back to Archer, the nightclub guy. The short one with the Ferrari. That would have been a fine life, right? Quiet. Pleasant.

Bullshit.

She wouldn't change a thing. (Okay, she would have figured out a way to get rid of Montserrat if she could.) But without the pain they'd gone through, she wouldn't have this. This beautiful eighteen-year-old girl in front of her, who was trying to explain to her parents what exactly went wrong in college.

Samantha squirmed in her seat. She fiddled with her cocktail straw. She shredded the wet napkin on her lap. "So the thing is, I was sleeping with this guy."

"What guy?" said Todd, already alarmed. "You had a boyfriend? A serious boyfriend? Why didn't you tell us before?"

"Relax, Dad," said Samantha. "Stop the presses, I'm not a virgin."

Todd looked wounded. Ellie felt for him. No one wanted to think about their kids' sex lives. *Ew.* Kids were like saints, sexless. That was the way it was supposed to be. To learn otherwise was anathema. Maybe it was easier for her since Sam was her step-daughter; she wondered if she'd be as cool about it when Giggy or the twins were Sam's age. Oh god, the twins. The hellions. She should get them vasectomies now.

"There was a guy? What about your girlfriend?" asked Ellie.

"I have a girlfriend now," said Sam patiently. "Not then."

"Oh, so you're bi?" Ellie perked up. Now they were getting somewhere; she could work with this.

"Mom, we don't have labels now. We just—like whom we like. Some people call it pansexual," said Samantha.

"Oh, okay," Ellie said even though she didn't quite understand and it felt a bit like, wow, if you liked whom you liked, then whom did you like? Did you like *everybody*? Was that how the game was played these days? Intriguing.

"Anyway, so I was sleeping with Jordan, my lit professor."

"Wait, wait, wait—you were sleeping with your professor?" Todd asked angrily. "Who is this asshole?"

"Dad, he's like a proctor, like an associate professor. He's like twenty-five or something," Sam said, as if that would mollify him.

And it did. Todd relaxed a little.

"Still, isn't that against the rules? Having an affair with your students?" Ellie asked. She hadn't gone to college, but she knew there were rules about this sort of thing.

Sam shrugged. "Anyway, that's not the point. I dumped him for Sofia. But he was obsessed with me, and accused me of plagiarism, which is against the honor code. We went up to the Honor Board, but he won, and the punishment is an automatic F in all my classes."

"Plagiarism?" Todd echoed.

"He said Sofia wrote my term paper because she'd taken his class last year and he recognized certain thesis statements and stuff."

Todd leaned forward, hands on his knees. "And did she?"

"No! Of course not! I would never!" Sam looked righteously indignant. Ellie almost believed it.

"Sam," she said sternly. "Did you cheat?"

Sam twiddled her thumbs and bit her lip. "I mean, technically . . ."

Todd slapped his forehead. "I don't believe it!"

"Dad! It was, like, nothing. You don't know how stressful it is. And I was working on her laptop. I was using her paper as a guide, but I got confused which was hers and which was mine. I didn't *mean* to."

Ellie crossed her arms and frowned. "*I'm* confused. If it was just one class, how did you end up with all Fs?"

"That's the policy; when you're found guilty on Honor Board, all your grades are affected," Sam said, pulling at a strand of her newly short hair.

"Well, that's not fair!" said Ellie.

Todd shushed her. "Go on, Sam."

"That's it." Sam shrugged. "That's the whole story."

"So your grades were fine?" asked Todd. "You actually weren't flunking out?"

"No, of course not! I was fine, until Jordan got involved. And he wouldn't have cared except he wanted revenge."

"If the Honor Board reverses their decision, then you can stay?" asked Ellie. "Is that how it works?"

"It would help, because, um, all this stress has affected my grades, and with all my Fs from last semester, my average is pretty low. I could get kicked out permanently," said Sam, looking anguished. "I was hoping not to have to tell you guys."

Todd took his daughter's hands in his. "We're glad you did. You know you can tell us anything. We're going to take care of this. You're not going anywhere. It's not your fault."

"Mean Celine is on the board at Stanford," Ellie suddenly remembered. She would have to confess Sam's secrets of course, and she would have to grovel. But she would do anything for her child, even going so far as to admit that said child was not perfect. Mean Celine was a friend, despite the label. "Don't worry, you won't be going anywhere. And that professor is fired!"

Sam threw herself into Ellie's arms. "Thanks, Mom. I knew you would fix it."

Ellie patted her daughter on her back. "Of course I will." She caught Todd's eyes over Sam's shoulders.

Thank you, he mouthed.

She nodded.

Ellie left Sam and Todd to themselves, since Todd wanted to talk to his daughter about the dangers of falling for older men, and what exactly constituted plagiarism. Ellie had to find Mean Celine and get this straightened out as soon as possible.

But instead of finding her friend, she bumped into a familiar face. One she hadn't seen in more than twenty years.

"Hey, stranger, there you are. Happy birthday," he said.

"Hey!" she said, trying to keep her voice light. "You made it!"

Part Three

JUST DESSERTS

THIRTY-ONE

Hell Hath No Fury

October 19
Twenty-Four Years Ago
11:45 P.M.

The bitch kissed her man. When Mish got mad, the voice in her head sounded like an angry, accusatory talk-show host riling up her guests in front of a hungry audience. She had played it cool at the party and had basically mauled her boyfriend to make him forget about kissing that slut. But inside, she was steaming.

"Hey, you okay?" asked Brooks, when Leo had left. The two of them were still sitting in the car alone. This was so not what she had planned for the evening. They were supposed to show Leo a good time, because it was her birthday, but that didn't include kissing the birthday girl.

She turned away.

"I didn't want to kiss her, it was just a dare; you know I'm crazy about you, babe," Brooks said, putting his chin on her shoulder and nuzzling her neck.

She pushed him away. "Liar."

"God, you can be such a cunt sometimes," he spat.

"Fuck you," she said, wiggling away and wrenching the door open.

"Fuck you too," he said as she slammed the door closed.

She watched him drive away angrily, and felt vindicated. Good, let him feel it. From the corner of her eye, she saw Leo walk toward her house and pretend that she didn't hear them fighting.

Happy birthday, bitch.

THIRTY-TWO

Old Dames

October 19
The Present
11:45 P.M.

It was so strange, seeing him again after all these years. It was like all the years melted away. He even sounded the same, if he didn't look exactly like he did before. Everything came back in a rush—that night, what happened, what happened next, what happened after that. The things you forget. She remembered shopping without paying. What a little thief she had been back then! What would her kids say if they knew? How could she explain her hardscrabble childhood to her spoiled little princes and princesses? What did they understand of poverty, of not having enough, of always being lesser? It wasn't just about money either. It was like, back then, they had been starved of everything—love, attention, care, even decency. How could she explain what she'd done? What would Todd say? What would Todd think?

But she had to put that out of her mind for now. Had to put him out of her mind. That was the past, and he was the past.

"Go get a drink! The bar's back there!" she told him. "I'll see you in a bit!" Did he still drink? He used to drink like a fish. They all did, but particularly him.

What did he remember? Did he remember that night?

It didn't matter. This was about now. About her daughter.

She was still just Celine when they first met. Ellie couldn't remember when she heard the "Mean" nickname or who had started calling her that. She was just Celine Barry, just another mom at Glenwood Prep, where they had just enrolled Sam in seventh grade. It was parent orientation, and Ellie stood out in the sea of puffy black tech vests, thin, ribbed turtlenecks, jeans, and status clogs. Welcome to the West Side. Ellie had just come from a meeting with her designers. She was wearing a cowboy hat and a fringed leather jacket over her white tank top, tight motocross jeans, and her Valentino Rockstud stilettos. She was easily twenty years younger than all the moms. Okay, fifteen. Ten.

She was sexy, and Brentwood did not do sexy.

But Celine, in a headband, padded vest, and Hunter boots, found her amusing. "I'm Celine, Alex's mom," she'd said, introducing herself to Ellie, who was standing alone, unsure of where to go. She'd never been a mom at a private school before. Montserrat was supposed to be here, but no one could find her. Todd was at work, of course. She had work too, but it was an unspoken agreement between them. Ellie dealt with the kids. Todd dealt with the network. Ellie did everything else.

"Ellie," said Ellie. "I'm Sam's mom. Well, stepmom."

"Is that right?"

"We just moved from New York," she explained. "At least I did. Todd's been here. But this is a new school for Sam."

"Sam . . . Samantha Stinson? Is that your daughter?"

"Yes!" said Ellie, relieved.

"Alex talks about Sam all the time; how wonderful to meet you."

It turned out Sam was Alex's favorite friend and since Alex was Celine's favorite child (she had four and Alex was the youngest), it was only natural that Ellie became Celine's favorite mom. And even if things weren't the same between the girls now, it didn't mean things had to change between the moms. Although of course, it had. They just weren't as close as they used to be. They used to gossip about the girls endlessly. But that had ended, and for a while Ellie was worried the friendship was over. But Celine was still at the party, she had made her appearance, and she didn't have to. Celine didn't have to be anywhere she didn't want to be. She wanted to be there, because she was still Ellie's friend.

Husbands could lie, they could cheat, they could die, but in the end, you had your girlfriends. Ellie had never been much of a girl's girl; she'd had a best friend when she was in high school but never anyone as close as the two of them had been. She was friendly with the model crew of her generation, the girls who used to run the circuit like she did—St. Barts, Aspen, St. Tropez, Palm Beach—just another girl getting a ride on the private jet and paying for the ride with a ride of her own. At least she'd married her ride—Archer. It bonded you, being young in a sea of gray money. She was used to flying solo, and that hadn't changed—much. She wasn't particularly close to any of the other moms, just Celine.

I knew you would fix it, Sam had said.

Thank you, Todd had mouthed.

How would she fix this? By being Celine's friend, it was already a fait accompli.

"Celine!" she said, finding her friend at the entrance and dropping the nickname for once.

"Cupcake!"

"I need to talk to you."

"Sure, honey, what's up?" asked Celine, who was holding her Judith Leiber clutch in a way that made Ellie suspicious.

"Are you leaving?" she accused. "It's not even midnight!"

Celine shrugged.

Ellie wanted to whine more to convince Celine to stay for the drag queens and the second after-party, to see the hotel suite that had been turned into a hookah lounge. But she knew once Celine was done, she was done. She had little time to explain.

"So, it's about Sam."

Celine nodded. "Uh-huh."

"And Stanford."

Celine raised an eyebrow.

This was hard. This was humiliating. Her perfect child. Her one perfect child who was not so perfect after all. But she did it. She told Celine the whole story, about the affair and the plagiarism and the Honor Board and the academic probation. "So, isn't that wrong? I mean, he was sleeping with her! A student! He had a motive. He was jealous and he wanted to get her into trouble."

But Celine didn't say anything. She just chewed on her lip. "Hmmm, that's going to be a dean issue."

"Dean?"

"Dean of studies. He'd have to make the call. And we'd have to prove that it was malicious on the professor's part, maybe even get him fired. It'll be a fight," said Celine, and she had a pugnacious look in her eye, the one she used to strong-arm benefactors into writing six-figure checks to her causes.

"We'll fight. It's Sam."

"Who had an affair with her professor and whose girlfriend wrote her term paper."

"She says she didn't," said Ellie hotly. "She swears she didn't cheat." It was a stretch. Sam had definitely crossed the line, but hadn't the professor done the same? Who was guilty? Who was innocent? Maybe no one, so why should her child pay for her mistake?

Celine sighed. "Do you know how easy it is to fake a term paper these days? Who knows what happened? Maybe she didn't or maybe she did."

It was exactly what Ellie was thinking, but she took umbrage anyway. "Are you blaming my kid?"

"No, I'm just laying it out for you. It'll be a battle; are you ready? Is Sam ready for that?"

Ellie nodded. They would do anything for their kid. Of course they would. They always had. "You can help, right? You'll make this go away? Sam can't be expelled from Stanford. Oh my god."

"I can talk to some people," said Celine. "But you know who you have to get on your side?"

"Who?"

"Blake," said Celine.

"Blake?" Her lips curled. "Why?"

"His new boyfriend is the dean of studies at Stanford. He was just telling me about him," said Celine. "I'll talk to the board, you talk to Blake. Make sure he gets his boyfriend to open up the case against Sam again, and make a new judgment. He'll do it if you ask."

"Can't *you* ask?" said Ellie jokingly.

Celine smiled. "Come on, Ellie. You love Blake."

"Do I?"

Her friend patted her cheek. "It's okay. It'll be okay. We'll take care of it. But you have to talk to Blake. I can only do so much." She placed her champagne glass on the nearest surface.

"You're really leaving?"

"Yes, wheels up in fifteen."

Ellie pouted. The evening was just getting started. She knew she had to usher Celine out the back way, lest other people get ideas and start to leave en masse. Her party could not end early. She would not let it.

"Come this way. I think your driver is parked over in back."

THIRTY-THREE

No Fury

October 20
Twenty-Four Years Ago
12:00 A.M.

There was no one home when Mish arrived, but that wasn't surprising. Mom was probably out with her sister; the two of them often found their way to the nearby tavern after their shifts at the factory, and her father was probably still at Sparkle.

She didn't even think of him as "Dad." Mostly, she called him nothing. He'd been gone her entire childhood; he was a stranger who was hardly ever around. And when he was around, he was surly, and drunk, or angry and drunk, or quiet and drunk.

Everyone said she looked like him, which she hated. She wished she looked more like her mom, who'd been a total knockout until the world wore her down. Mom had even won one of those beauty contests back in the day, and there were rumors that she had once dated Donald Overton; wasn't that ironic? If they had gotten together, she and Brooks would be brother and sister.

Mish was annoyed, and so drunk she couldn't walk straight. The whole day had started out so promising, but had ended in a fight. Her head hurt and she was dizzy. The minute she got to her room, she fell on her bed and passed out cold.

The sound of a car engine roaring up and shutting off woke her. Mish sat up and pulled aside the curtains to look out the window. There was someone going into Leo's house. A guy. It was dark, and she couldn't see who it was, or what car he was driving, but she knew, deep down in her gut, who it was.

THAT FUCKER, thought Mish. HE CAME BACK TO FINISH.

He'd gotten a little taste, and now he wanted the whole enchilada. The two of them had been making eyes at each other all night. Mish couldn't get the sight of them kissing out of her head. Brooks had placed his hand on Leo's cheek, the way he always did on hers. It was like he'd traded her for her best friend, like she was replaceable, as if the two of them were interchangeable with each other.

She quickly put on her jeans and sneakers and ran out the door, her heart pounding. She couldn't quite believe he had the audacity to do this; in a way, she'd believed him when he said he loved her. She thought she was special. He was the only one who made her feel that way, other than Leo of course.

Her best friend with her boyfriend. It was unforgivable. She would shame them, she would scream, she would cry and she would hit, punch, claw—she pictured nails drawing blood— she would hurt them. She would. She would make them hurt as much as she hurt right now, all twisted and sad and angry and shaking from betrayal.

The door was unlocked, and she let herself in.

She heard the bed creak, muffled sounds, like kissing. Her blood began to boil. She had caught them in the act! She could picture it all too clearly, Leo underneath, Brooks heaving. His lips on hers, his body on hers, and he was hers, not Leo's.

FUCKING SLUT!

She took a deep breath, steeled herself, and threw open the door.

THIRTY-FOUR

Old Flames

October 20
The Present
12:00 A.M.

Y *ou love Blake.* Do I? How much did Celine know? Did she
just guess or had Ellie spilled the beans once? Ellie thought
that maybe she had told her friend about her and Blake. Oh, Celine was right about that. She had loved him once. Very briefly.
But she had loved him all the same.

She had to find Blake to talk to him, at least this way she
wouldn't have to talk to *him* just yet. She had no desire to rehash
the past. If only she hadn't told so many people about her party.

Anyway, Blake. It was right after she and Archer had broken
up the first time. Blake came to take her out. Blake was always
around back then. He was such a handsome thing. Todd once
accused her of sleeping with everyone they'd met. All because
she'd admitted she'd slept with Jared Leto when Todd introduced
her to him at the Emmys! He was so jealous about that one. And
oh my god, it was just Jared Leto. Everyone slept with Jared Leto,

and Jared slept with everyone. (And he didn't have a small penis; she just told Todd that to make him feel better.)

She didn't sleep with everyone she knew. Or did she?

Ellie had to admit Todd was right about Blake. They'd had a fling. But did her husband have to know everything about her past? What did it matter whom she'd slept with if she wasn't sleeping with them anymore?

Anyway, Blake. He had come over to the apartment when he'd heard she was depressed after the breakup with Archer.

"Come on, let's go out," he said. "You can't just stay here, moping."

Archer was in Spain again. He was always in Spain. And she'd just found out he was fucking the housekeeper. Only Archer would have a hot housekeeper. Only Archer would take their housekeeper to Spain for the weekend.

She'd thrown one of her shoes at Archer when he left. "FUCKER!"

Why did she think he would be faithful? Why would anyone think she was enough? Why couldn't anyone love her the way she deserved to be loved? Would anyone ever love her the way she loved them? She loved Archer, but it didn't matter. He loved his freedom.

Blake came over and kicked her. Lightly.

She was lying on the bed, unable to move. The place was a mess. (See: housekeeper. Ibiza.)

"Come on, get yourself up; it's just Archer."

"What do you mean?"

"No one mopes around for Archer," Blake said, sounding particularly posh right then. She'd always loved his British accent.

"Why not?"

"Because," said Blake. "That's just what he does. He slept with my sister. Did I tell you? She was mad for him. But he dumped her too. He dumps everyone."

"We. Are. Married," she told him. "It's different."

Blake shrugged. "Tell yourself that."

Blake was her age. Archer was old. Blake was fun. He had a lot of sisters. One of them was Archer's age. That's how they knew Blake.

She couldn't remember the first time she met him, only that he was always around and always up for another drink. Blake Burberry. This handsome, skinny boy.

"Come on, Elle, get yourself up. There's a party. I need a drink," he said.

She dragged herself out of the bed. She put on something to wear and she went out with him. They went to Groucho, then Annabel's, and ended up dancing next to a stuffed giraffe at Loulou's at 5 Hertsford Street. The place was packed with royals and billionaires and socialites, her favorite kind of party. It cheered her up. She was glad to be out.

"Thanks, man," she said, punching him on the arm.

He was so pretty back then.

"You're so pretty," she told him, lying in his arms the next morning. Right, they'd tumbled into bed at dawn. It seemed only polite.

"*You're* so pretty," he drawled.

She looked at him. He had saved her. He had pulled her from

the funk. Sanjay had saved her too. (Literally. Who knows what that crazy sheik would have done?) But Blake had saved her heart. Archer broke her heart. She had loved him and he had broken her heart, but Blake had pieced it back together. They spent the week going to art galleries and shopping and ordering seafood towers at Scott's.

Their favorite pastime was to go to Harvey Nick's and try on clothes and critique each other's choices. Blake dressed like an English dandy, all Berluti suede jackets and Drake's scarves.

"You have a good eye," he said. "What are you going to do?"

Okay, so maybe he wasn't that much of a douche all the time. Maybe he had even helped her figure out her company.

"I don't know. I was thinking something in fashion," she said. "I have an interview with Chanel next week."

"You should have a brand," he said. "And you should be the face of it." At last, years later—after she left Chanel after five years to work for Michael Kors for three—she did exactly that.

But back in London, when they were young, those two heady weeks. "I love you," she whispered, after he'd rolled off her.

"Hmmm," said Blake, now rolling a cigarette. "Pardon? Didn't quite catch that."

"Nothing." She didn't repeat it. But she had said it and she meant it. She loved him. It was why she could never get rid of him later.

It didn't last. He started dating someone else. A beautiful boy.

He was bisexual, but she was the only girl he'd ever been with, or at least that's what he said. She liked to think she was special, but who knew.

He told her as much. He cared for her, but it was over. He had gotten her out of her funk, and she was on her feet now, and he had moved on. He would dance with her at her wedding to Todd a few years later.

Blake Burberry. Still single, still searching. She wondered if he would ever settle down, or would he grow up to be just like Archer, the perennial bachelor?

Blake was sprawled in the corner, holding court, his long legs on their Minotti couch, holding a glass of red wine. "Relax," he said when he saw her face. "I'll pay for it if it stains."

"You better!"

He dismissed his minions. "What's up?" It was only then that she noticed he was wearing an ascot. She tamped down the slight irritation.

"Celine said your new boyfriend is the dean of studies at Stanford," she said.

"Yeah," he said. "I'm getting intellectual in my old age." He smirked.

"Good," she said.

"Why?"

"I need a favor."

THIRTY-FIVE

Two Can Keep a Secret

October 20
Twenty-Four Years Ago
12:00 A.M.

It was exactly midnight. Her birthday was over. She was officially sixteen, and had been kissed by the two people who had celebrated with her. But now her best friend hated her; she'd seen the look in Mish's eyes at the end of the evening. Mish was not only her best friend, but her only friend, the only reason Leo had someone to celebrate with—and Leo had stabbed her in the back. It wasn't her fault, she told herself. It was just a game!

Except it wasn't, and Leo knew it, and Mish knew it, and the only one who was clueless about what was going on was Brooks. She didn't even want Brooks. She just wanted—someone who was just for her. Someone who made her feel special.

That someone was Mish. She was all she had and now Leo didn't have her either.

Arnold was supposed to come over when the club closed, but

he probably wouldn't. He didn't really like her; he was just being nice. He was letting her down easy. She was nothing, she was nobody. She was the kind of girl someone like Dave Griffin could use like a tissue and then forget about. Arnold wasn't coming over.

She let herself inside the house and noticed her mom had left a message on the machine. *Happy birthday, sweetie. I'm so sorry I'm not home yet. They asked me if I could night-manage the swing shift, so I won't be home until five in the morning. I left your cake in the fridge. We can eat it tomorrow?*

Leo deleted the phone message. She opened the card, and a twenty-dollar bill slipped out. Wow, that was even less than she was expecting. Things must be pretty dire.

She yawned, changed into her sweatpants and an old T-shirt, checked that the front door was locked, and went to bed.

The hand on her thigh didn't wake her up completely, but she knew, almost immediately, who was in the bed with her.

"Shhhh," he whispered.

She squirmed. Should she pretend to be asleep, like before? That's what she did, ever since it started, after the first time, when he'd begun to come over at night.

Just pretend it didn't happen.

Just pretend she wasn't awake.

Just pretend she didn't know what was happening.

She shut her eyes. She could feel his breath on her neck, and she cringed, repelled, her entire body paralyzed and cold.

Leo closed her eyes and felt the tears on her cheeks even though she didn't realize she was crying. The first time it happened, he'd been looking for Leo's mom. He came over in the middle of the day, right after he'd gotten out of prison. He was a handsome man, smooth and strong.

"Hey, your mom around?" he'd asked.

"She got a job, she's at work," said Leo. She didn't pay attention to him; he was just Mish's dad, the guy across the street, the guy who just got out of jail.

"So you're Leo, huh?"

Leo looked up. "Yeah."

"You know, your mom and I used to date, before she married your dad." He smirked, crossing his arms against his chest so she could see the tattoos snaking up his forearms. There was one of a heart, one of a snake, and one of Mish's face as a baby. She decided the tattoos were butt-ugly and looked away.

"Okay," she said, in a tone that meant she didn't care in the least.

"You ever know your dad?"

"Nope."

"Yeah, well, me neither," he said, barking a laugh. He sized her up keenly. "Want a beer?"

Leo looked up. "You're serious?"

"Yeah. Why not?"

That first time, he just brought her a beer. That's all they did. They sat and drank, and she'd never had a beer before; it was kind of bitter and she didn't like the taste, so the next time, he brought her a bunch of wine coolers. Mish was working at Sears, so Leo had her afternoons to herself, and she started looking forward to his visits. He was funny, and kind of cool, and he paid more attention to her than her mom, who was always working.

It was later that the other stuff happened. The first time, it was a surprise, and she hadn't even been able to understand what was happening until it was too late, and she'd lost her virginity. Funny thing, losing your virginity; it sounded like she'd misplaced it somewhere, like she'd lost it at the mall, or dropped it on the street.

In reality, it had been taken from her without her consent, without her agreeing to it, and she didn't even understand that it was something you could agree to, that it was something you gave away, not something that was taken from you unexpectedly. Then she thought she was pregnant. That was the worst part. But then she got her period and everything was okay again, or as much as it could be.

He would come over a lot, at night, when he knew her mother was working at the restaurant. Sometimes she would pretend to be asleep. Sometimes she couldn't pretend, but she knew she musn't cry out, and musn't tell anyone. It was a secret, a dirty, disgusting secret, and it made her feel disgusting and ashamed and gross and she hated herself for letting it happen; it was all her fault, all her fault, all her fault. And if she told anybody, they'd say the same thing.

She never, ever, ever, ever told Mish.

No, not today, she pleaded in her mind. No, please, not on her birthday, of all days. No, she didn't want this. She never had. She just wanted to sleep, just wanted to dream of another life.

She opened her eyes.

"Surprise! Happy birthday, girl!" He was staring down at her, as if she was the most beautiful thing he'd ever seen. Just like that first afternoon. Just like all the nights after.

She saw her face reflected in his eyes, her fear and her rage, and she moved, so fast she couldn't believe it; she was a blur, she was all motion and fury. She knew this was going to happen, she expected it. She grabbed the gun underneath her bed and pointed it at him. The gun she'd hidden there the day after he'd visited the last time. His own gun that she'd stolen from him.

"Hey now! Whoa! Hold on there!" he said, trying to scramble away and holding up his hands in surrender.

"Don't touch me! Never touch me again!" she screamed.

Quick as lightning, he lunged, grabbing it out of her hand. He was so terribly strong, he pinned her down, but she was strong too, with fury and spite, and now they were struggling with it, rolling off the bed, rolling against each other, and she held on to the gun; she would never let go.

She had the gun in her hand, her finger on the trigger. She saw his face, the shock and the fear. This was it. This was the last time.

She had the upper hand, for once. Everything was going to change. Everything was going to be different. All she had to do was shoot.

But just then, the door banged open.

That split second.

That was all it took.

He saw his chance. He wrestled the gun away from her, turned it the other way, so that it pointed away from his stomach and into her chest.

The gun fired. One shot. That was all it took.

There was a scream.

Who was screaming?

It wasn't her.

She couldn't make a sound. Because her mouth was full of blood. And it wasn't her voice. She wasn't the one who called him that . . . who called him—

"DADDY!"

THIRTY-SIX

So Many Old Flames

October 20
The Present
12:15 A.M.

Ellie peeped back into the party room. Yep, there he was. The one and only Brooks Overton, looking out of place for once in his life. She'd forgotten she'd invited him. He'd sent her a friend request on Facebook a few months back, right before reunion, and she'd accepted. She wondered if she should tell him about the texts she'd received earlier in the evening. She wondered if Brooks was still in touch with *him*. The one who'd sent her all the texts earlier. Not that they'd ever been close friends, but things were different now with social media and all those things that sort of connected people but not really. How many times had she promised old friends from Portland that she would see them if they were ever in town? So many times. How many times had she seen them? Zero.

Oh my god, Brooks, of all people, was fat. Fatter than Todd. So much fatter. She'd really given her husband a hard time, when in reality, he'd been so skinny before that the extra forty pounds weren't terrible on him. Whereas someone ate Brooks and was now wearing his face.

She picked up Celine's barely touched champagne glass and walked over to him. It wasn't as if she could ignore him all night.

"Where are you staying?" she asked.

"The Hilton. I have points," he said.

She never knew what to say when people said they used points. Condolences, maybe? Her dearest friend, her business manager, never stayed anywhere he had to pay; the man traveled on Marriot, American Express, Hyatt, Hilton, and Starwood points. It would be kind of sad if it wasn't also endearing.

"Mishon told me about the party, said I should stop by. I saw her at reunion," he said. "We missed you."

"It was Fashion Week. I couldn't make it," she said. She had spent the weekend in Las Vegas, at the trade show, selling units like crazy. She'd had no time for a high school reunion.

Brooks was balding too. That golden mop of hair was gone. Now he looked like any ordinary middle-aged white guy. No one would believe he used to be beautiful. Oh, the ravages of time. She fought against it, every step of the way, with medical procedures and her thousand-dollar eye creams, but some people couldn't or didn't, and the loss of such beauty made her sad.

"You look exactly the same," he said. "Gorgeous as always."

"Oh, I don't know about that; you're too kind."

"Look at you now." He whistled. "Is that a real Damien Hirst?"

"Yeah, we bought it at auction. My husband . . . collects." She was richer now than Brooks and his family had ever been. She laughed sometimes when she thought about how young and naïve she had been, how little she knew of the world, how much he and his family had impressed her. She had lapped them and more.

"You know I turned forty two years ago."

"Yeah? What'd you do to celebrate?"

He shrugged, took another pull of his beer. "Went out to dinner with the wife and kids."

"Nice," she said.

"Yeah, it was okay," he said. "Nothing like this."

"As my husband says, not everyone needs this," she said. What a lie! For Todd's birthday, they went on safari and then a river cruise down the Nile with a group that included the Beckhams and the Bransons—Sanjay had invited them.

Brooks nodded.

Ellie tried to keep her voice light. "So how was reunion? Was everyone there?"

"Yeah, it was all right. Stacey was there; she's married, two kids; they still live up in Arlington."

Ellie tittered. "Of course she does." It was exactly as she'd predicted.

"Olivia was there; she's a lawyer in the Bay Area. Divorced. Um, who else? Dave Griffin; he lives in Chicago, still single. He works in insurance."

"I know," she snorted. "He works for us." It was a revenge hire, as she still remembered how rude Dave had been in high school. Ugh, Dave. Gross. It was satisfying hearing him grovel to her and her husband on the phone as he tried to sell them more insurance. She kept him around like a talisman, like a chieftain, using her old oppressors as victims. What was the line? You will work for us someday. Well, that someday came to Dave Griffin.

"Oh," said Brooks. "Well, Andie's in rehab, for the sixth time."

"I can't say I'm surprised," she said coldly, remembering the condescending senior.

"Deacon's a tax attorney. You kept in touch with Mishon."

"Yeah. She's pretty much the only person I still know from high school," said Ellie.

Brooks smiled. "You have any kids?"

"I have four; my eldest is at Stanford," she said, out of habit. "Then another girl, and two boys."

"I have three, all boys."

She hoped he wouldn't show her a picture, but he did anyway. She pretended to be interested in his bland offspring. What was he doing here? Ugh.

Her husband walked up. "Todd, this is Brooks. I told you about him earlier," said Ellie. "He was the one who was texting me," she said pointedly.

Todd offered his hand, assessed the stranger.

Brooks took it warmly. "Hey, man, I used to be madly in love with your wife."

"Weren't we all," said Todd with a smirk.

"Gee, thanks, I think," said Ellie.

"Come on, let me get you a drink," said Todd.

Ellie excused herself as her phone was ringing again, and this time, she wanted to make sure she actually got to talk to Harry.

"Ellie!" he said, his voice carrying over the scratchy line.

"I'm so sorry; it's my party and the reception out in the desert is the worst."

"No problem. I was on a plane, so I couldn't call you, and we just landed," he explained.

"So what's going on? Should I be worried?"

"Well, I have to tell you that we're not doing the deal."

"Oh." Ellie felt as if the ground underneath her had just swallowed her whole. She was done.

"Yes, we ran the numbers and it didn't make sense."

"Right. Well. Okay. Fine. Thanks for letting me know," she said.

"Ellie—I'm so sorry . . ." he said, but she'd already hung up. What was there to talk about? She didn't want to ruin her mood any more than it was ruined.

Ruined.

She always imagined a girl in a white dress in the rain with mascara running down her cheeks. RUINED.

She was RUINED.

She put her phone away. She was calculating sums in her head, coming up short in every scenario. What would she tell Todd, how would she break it to the kids? So she really had no time for Brooks right now, who had made his way back to her to make another declaration she didn't need to hear, while Todd was still at the bar, waiting for their drinks.

"I shouldn't have let you go so easily. I know I made a mistake, back then," he said.

Ellie sighed. She had no intention of walking down memory lane, but perhaps it was inevitable. "Mmm," she said.

"I was crazy about you," he said. "You broke my heart."

"We were young" was all she said.

"So young," he agreed. "You ever think about that night?"

"What night?" she asked, although she knew full well the night in question.

"You know. The night of Stacey's birthday party."

"Oh yeah," she said. "That night. Hey, about that night, you know who texted me today?"

"Who?"

"You'll never guess."

THIRTY-SEVEN

If One of Them Is Dead

October 20
Twenty-Four Years Ago
12:15 A.M.

ADDY, WHAT ARE YOU DOING?!"

Mish stood in the doorway, her face frozen in horror. That was not Brooks in Leo's bedroom. It was never Brooks, and it wasn't Brooks now. She stared at the bed, the rumpled sheets, and she knew. She knew exactly where her father spent his nights.

Now her father was holding a gun and Leo was on the floor, in a pool of blood. Leo's eyes were glazed and she wasn't moving. Leo was dead. Oh my god, Leo was dead. Leo was dead. Leo was dead and it was all her fault. Mish knew it was. She knew.

She'd banged open the door, and she'd seen. She'd seen Leo with the gun, Leo with the upper hand, but the two of them had turned to her, her father and Leo, turning to the door to see what was happening, and in that moment, her dad had grabbed the gun from her friend and shot her dead.

"DON'T MOVE!" her father yelled.

Mish froze.

Her father held a gun. Her father had killed her best friend. Her father had been . . . it was unthinkable. Her father had been having sex with Leo. Her father. Her father. Her father told her not to move. Her father was looking at her, wondering what she would do.

Mish knew what she had to do. She took a picture. She was still holding her camera; she'd run out of her room so angry she forgot she still had it slung over her shoulder. The flash startled both of them.

"WHAT THE HELL!" her father yelled.

She had to get out of there.

She ran.

"COME BACK HERE!" he screamed. He jumped from the bed, still holding the gun, and lunged for her, his fingers skimming her long blond hair as he fell.

He skittered in the blood, then tripped on the broken tile, slipped on it, just as Leo had that morning. Except instead of going ass-down, he fell at the wrong angle.

Slipped on the tile, and he went down hard, right on his head.

Mish heard the crack.

Just like the punch Leo's dad had given that guy. One punch. Fell at the wrong angle. Hit the ground hard and died.

Her dad fell and hit his head.

The crack echoed throughout the tiny house.

Mish didn't scream. She just watched.

Her father fell at an unnatural angle; he had hit his head and now he wasn't moving. He had killed Leo and now he was dead as well.

When the front door opened, she almost screamed.

But it was only Arnold.

He looked at her and he looked at her dad sprawled on the floor, and through the doorway to Leo's room, to Leo, dead on the floor.

He didn't say a word. He just nodded. He was cool, like he dealt with this kind of thing all the time.

"Is he . . . is he . . . ?" she asked as Arnold leaned over her father's body.

Arnold shook his head. "He's still breathing."

Shit.

"We could call an ambulance," he said.

Mish nodded. They had to call an ambulance, didn't they? That's what people did when they saw all this blood, all this violence. But if they were going to call an ambulance, they would have done it already.

Arnold looked at Mish. Mish looked away. They stayed like that for a long time, the only sound the ticking clock on the wall.

They let him bleed out.

Finally, he stopped breathing.

"He was hurting her," she told Arnold. "He hurt her."

Arnold nodded. "Yeah, I kind of figured that. She kind of hinted something weird was going on. She didn't want to be home alone. Not tonight."

"Is that why you're here?"

"Yeah. Except I was too late." Arnold looked down at the dead man. "He's gone now. He was still your dad. I'm sorry."

"I'm not," said Mish, and she kicked the dead man's shin, hard. He was definitely dead. He was gray now, and getting cold. Now they could call an ambulance. "He was an asshole."

THIRTY-EIGHT

After

October 20
Twenty-Four Years Ago
12:30 A.M.

What is dead may never die. It would be years before Mish would become a *Game of Thrones* fan, but later, when she thought about what happened next, she would think of the wights, the dead zombies coming to life to attack whatever poor soul was close enough to devour. Arnold had gone to get a towel, and some water, because she was still shaking. But just as she turned away from her father, just as she hung up with 911, just after she had finally called the ambulance—that was when she felt a hand grasp her ankle.

"Urrgggh." Her father was alive.

The bastard was alive.

His eyes were mean. "This is all your fault."

She grit her teeth and shook her head. "Shut the fuck up!"

"It should have been you," he whispered. "It should have been you."

Mish looked at Leo, lying dead on the floor. Beautiful, vibrant

Leo who had just turned sixteen years old. Her father was telling the truth. It should have been her. She'd seen the way her father sized them up, the two of them, when he got back from jail.

"Pretty little things," he'd said, his eyes taking way too long over both of them, their long legs sprawled on the couch. They were twelve years old.

She'd known what he wanted.

Mish told him that Leo's mom worked late nights, that Leo was always alone. But she hadn't known what would happen after she told him, did she? Not really. She just hinted. She just let him look elsewhere. So that she wouldn't have to find him in her bed.

Now he was clawing at her ankle, and he was strong enough to pull her down. She screamed. Arnold ran back with a glass of water and he yelled when he saw her father alive and clawing at her, and they all three saw it at the same time.

The gun.

The gun he'd shot Leo with, it was still there, on the floor, not too far from his right hand.

She had to get the gun before he did.

Get the gun.

But no, her father was there first. He was so fast for a dead guy. He grabbed it and cocked it and pointed it right at her.

"It should have been you!" he raged.

He was insane. He was crazy. He had killed Leo and now he was going to kill her too. She was going to die and she'd never even left this stupid neighborhood.

"No!" she screamed and she wondered why no one else was

here, why the whole neighborhood was silent. It was like they were the only people on the planet.

Her father had his gun and it was aimed at her.

She was going to die.

Everything slowed down. For the rest of her life, she would remember it like an operatic ballet. Movies had it right sometimes; sometimes your life narrowed down to those few seconds.

The gun was in her face.

Then it wasn't.

Somehow, Arnold slapped it away; he slapped her father's hand away, and Mish caught the gun.

She had it in her hand now. It was still warm, and so heavy. It had killed her best friend already.

She had the gun in hand, and without thinking, without hesitation, she shot her father straight through the temple.

Now he was dead.

Soon, there were lights flashing on the window, but it wasn't an ambulance. It was a BMW. It was Brooks.

THIRTY-NINE

After After

October 20
Twenty-Four Years Ago
12:40 A.M.

S hit, is that your boyfriend? Shit!" said Arnold. "What are we going to do?"

Mish had to think fast. Brooks was here. What was he doing here? Was he coming back to see Leo? Was he? That fucking asshole. How much did he see? How much did he know? Did he see her shoot her dad?

"Get out of here!" she told Arnold. She gave him a shove. "I'll take care of him. You didn't see anything. You don't know anything."

"Mish . . ."

She closed her eyes. She didn't have time to argue right now. Right now, Leo was dead and she had just shot her father. "GO AWAY, ARNOLD! YOU DIDN'T SEE ANYTHING! I DON'T NEED YOUR HELP!"

"Fuck you, Mish," he said.

When she opened her eyes, she saw Arnold glaring at her, his eyes burning with hate. He knew her. He knew her dark heart. It was why she hated him, because Arnold knew who she really was. She despised him for knowing her.

"Fuck you, Arnold," she shot back. "What are you going to do? How can you help? You're just the fucking neighborhood loser. Go! You can't help me! Leave!"

Arnold shook his head and went out the back door, slamming it behind him.

She could hear Brooks outside. "Hey, man, what's up?"

Arnold didn't respond.

What was the story? What was she going to tell Brooks? How was she going to explain *this*?

She'd tell him the truth, or as much of the truth as she could tell. That she'd walked in on them, and her dad killed Leo. Then he killed himself. Right. Her dad had killed himself. Obviously.

That was the story. That was the story she'd tell for the rest of her life. And the first one to hear it was Brooks.

"HELP!" she screamed. "HELP! HELP ME! THEY'RE DEAD!"

Brooks burst through the door, confused. "What's going on?"

Then he saw. His face turned white and he backed away from her, but Mish was having none of that.

She collapsed in his arms. "Oh, Brooks, thank god! Thank god you're here!"

FORTY

First Comes Love

October 20
The Present
12:30 A.M.

It was so late. Ellie yawned. She was tired and she didn't know if she had the energy to go play bingo with a bunch of drag queens any time soon. Plus, Brooks was still here. He'd missed dinner and the soprano and the speeches, but he was here for a drink or two. He'd come by because he was at some boring business convention and she'd invited him, since he was in town, to her birthday party.

"So how do you know Michelle?" Todd asked genially, as he brought over a round of cocktails.

Brooks raised his eyebrows. "Mish didn't tell you?"

"Mish? You mean Mishon?" asked Todd, confused.

"Honey, *I'm* Mish," said Ellie, who'd grimaced at hearing her old nickname once more. No one called her that anymore. Mishon—who had once been Shona Silverstein—was the only Mish that Todd knew.

"Right," said Todd, after taking a sip of his drink, as if that wasn't important. It was just her past after all. "Anyway, how *do* you guys know each other? Is it a secret?" Todd joked.

"Sort of," Ellie mumbled.

Todd raised his eyebrows and gave Brooks a shrug. "Well, that's no surprise; she keeps everything from me."

"Ah, well, it's ancient history," said Brooks.

Todd grunted.

"We were married, Brooks and I," Ellie blurted. "Technically, he's my first husband. But it got annulled, so it doesn't count."

Todd took a long sip of his drink. "Well, that's a relief." Then they all laughed, because what else was there to say?

They had eloped that night. For some reason, it all made sense. To keep Brooks from talking about what he knew, if he knew anything. If he'd seen anything. If he'd heard anything. Had he? Would he ever tell if he had? It didn't matter, because you couldn't testify against your spouse, right? There was some kind of law that covered that.

"Let's get married!" she'd demanded. The ambulance would be on its way, and if not, Leo's mom would be there soon. They would take care of it. They didn't need to be around for that. She knew the sooner she could get out of there, the better.

"Are you serious?" He couldn't believe it.

"Yeah, I love you," she said.

"I love you too, but . . ."

"But what, Brooks?"

"Okay," he said. "Okay. When?"

"Tonight."

"But what about . . ." He gestured to the house, to everything that lay in there. So dead and so cold.

"It doesn't matter."

They would find them tomorrow anyway. What did it matter? And by tomorrow, she would be Mrs. Brooks Overton, and everything it promised. He would protect her. He had to do it. He was all she had now. She ran her fingers through his hair and kissed his forehead. "Please."

"Okay," he said.

"Is that a yes?"

"YES!"

They flew out to Mexico that very evening, Brooks putting the tickets on his dad's credit card, and were married by a sleepy clerk at the civic office the next morning. She had no idea why they'd gone to Mexico instead of Las Vegas, but they ended up in Tijuana. Brooks bought rings from a roadside stand selling cheap silver jewelry.

When they returned to Portland, all everyone could talk about was how Leo had been killed by a neighbor, that was all that was on the news, all that anyone cared about. No one asked where she and Brooks had been that night. No one cared. No one knew they were married. They kept it a secret, until Brooks told his parents right before graduation, that he was going to college and signing up for the married people dorm, and when they asked why on earth he was doing that, he confessed.

It was over quickly. His parents were lawyers; the marriage was annulled before the next semester even began. Brooks went off to college and she never saw him again.

She would have sat around heartbroken except by then, she had booked her first gig, in Tokyo, then London, and by the time she saw her eighteenth birthday, she had already met Archer, already hooked the bigger fish.

Brooks had been a blip, a mistake, a ghost, someone she never even thought about at all.

Todd excused himself to check on the caterers, who were packing up; only Victor was still working, and Madison was trying to get people to board the party bus to the next destination. Drag queens didn't wait for no one.

Brooks looked at her, as if studying her face. It had been a long time since they were together, alone. "I didn't speak to my parents for years," he told her. "I was so mad at them for what they did to us. I hated them for it."

"I didn't know."

"Yeah," he said.

She sighed. Poor Donald and Judy Overton. The worst thing had happened; some townie had married their golden boy. She still remembered the repulsed look on their faces when they found out, the truth behind their friendly smiles all those years.

"You know, I don't think I ever got over you," he said wistfully.

"Oh, Brooks, stop."

"I came tonight to tell you that."

"Well, I wish you hadn't," she said. "I'm not sixteen anymore. None of us are."

She looked at her phone. Another text from *him*. He was finally here.

Come out to the back, she typed. I'm by the bar. Brooks is here too.

FORTY-ONE

Old Flames (3)

October 20
The Present
12:45 A.M.

Brooks didn't want to stay to say hi. He had to go back to the convention, he said. It was good to see her, congrats on everything, truly. But he didn't need to shoot the shit; it's not like they were ever friends to begin with.

Brooks left and Ellie waited for her other guest. She saw him before he saw her. He looked exactly like he used to, with that long hair in his eyes, but skinny had turned to gaunt, and he looked a bit feral, skeletal. But at least he'd gotten his teeth fixed. He was still handsome, filthy-sexy, and she wondered if that was why she was so jealous that night, when he'd paid so much more attention to her friend than to her.

Because she'd loved him first.

Before Brooks, before Archer, before Todd.

There was Arnold.

They used to ride their bikes on the riverbank, and go hunt frogs together. They read comic books and wrote stories and sometimes when her dad was home between prison sentences and fighting with her mom, she would go over to Arnold's house and they would watch television. He was her first kiss and her first love.

But then his mom died, and he had to take care of his grandma, and his sister started turning tricks and dating sugar daddies, and he dropped out, and he started selling drugs. He shared them with her sometimes. They'd do poppers in the alley and laugh and laugh. He'd asked her to go to some party where he was working; it was the same party Leo wanted to go to but didn't, and that was where she'd met Brooks. Then it was all Brooks all the time and she forgot about Arnold.

Now he was all grown up just like her. He'd survived, just like her, made his way out of Woods Forest Park, just like her. Not too far, though; she heard he still lived around Portland. Never married, though. Some guys weren't the type.

"Hey," she said.

"Hey," he said. He smiled. "Happy birthday."

"Thanks."

Arnold had cleaned himself up. After that night, after she married Brooks, he went back to school. Something about that night shook him out of himself. He didn't want to end up like her dad, lying dead in a trailer somewhere. He didn't want that for himself. He got clean and he got out. He became a cop. He worked vice, just on the other side now.

She'd been scared at first, when she heard he was in law enforcement, but then nothing happened. He left her alone, until tonight. Why was he here? What did he want? What was he going to do with what he knew about what she'd done?

There was no statute of limitations on murder. Her father was a felon, and as much as she'd tried to run away from her past, it was always there, always there in front of her. Was that where she was going to end up? She supposed there were worse things than being poor.

"So what's going on? I don't hear from you for twenty years and now you show up on my birthday?" she asked.

"Is that a crime?" he asked.

"Fuck you," she said, laughing. "Seriously, why are you here?" She shuddered. He was the only one who knew what really happened that night. The only one who knew what she'd done. "Do you need money?"

Arnold tossed his cigarette into the bushes. He shook his head, amused. "You can keep your money, birthday girl."

"What, then? What do you want? Why are you here, Arnold?"

He shrugged. "I was feeling nostalgic. I heard about your party from Dani; she saw it on your Facebook page, wasn't hard to find your address, so I figured I'd come and say hey."

"Hey," she said.

"I miss her, you know. Leo."

"I do too. All the time," she said defensively.

They both were silent then, remembering the girl they used to know.

"Anyway," he said at last. "I came because I've got a present for you."

"You didn't have to."

"I think I did," he said. "I found it in an old storage unit."

"What is it?"

He brought it out. It was her bag from that night. She'd left it in Leo's room, in the pool of blood. She opened the bag, knowing what she would find. Her Polaroid camera and the photos. Leo. Her and Leo. Leo and Brooks. Leo and Arnold. Leo and Dave. Leo and her dad together. Her father reaching for the camera. Blood on the floor.

"Oh," she said. "Oh my god."

"It's yours." He yawned. "I thought you should have it. Destroy it, keep it, whatever."

She zipped up the bag. She would destroy it. Burn it in a big bonfire. The kids could roast marshmallows on it. "About that night," she said. "About what happened . . ."

"It wasn't your fault," Arnold said, waving it away, like it was nothing, like it never happened. "It never was."

Maybe he was right. Maybe it could stay in the past forever, where it belonged. She wasn't that person anymore. She hadn't been that person in a long time.

FORTY-TWO

Truth (2)

October 20
The Present
12:50 A.M.

Madison-and-Lex had been successful in corralling the guests onto the bus, although a few had excused themselves and were headed back to the hotel, which annoyed Ellie. She liked a captive audience, or maybe she should have moved the party up an hour, so that more people would end up at the club.

She found Todd in the back, smoking a joint with Sanjay.

"Your creepy ex-boyfriend still here?" he asked. "Excuse me, ex-husband?"

"Long story," said Ellie, rolling her eyes. She didn't tell him about Arnold. One ex was enough for the night.

"Uh-oh," said Sanjay. "Which one was he?"

"Fat bastard, looked like he came off a golf course," said Todd.

Sanjay snickered and passed the joint over. She took a hit and exhaled. "Nah, he left. I didn't tell him about the after-party."

"Good," said Todd.

"I should find Monica. We'll see you at the club," said Sanjay, who knew the rule for old friends was that old friends were the last to leave. He knew he wouldn't be allowed to go to bed until the sun came up.

"What's up?" asked Todd, since Ellie was just standing there, looking tense.

"The deal's off. Harry's company isn't buying Wild & West."

"Okay," he said.

"We're ruined. We won't make payroll, or the shipment, or anything. We can't keep it going, we're going to have to sell," she said. Somehow, knowing she wasn't going to prison made going bankrupt that much more palatable.

"So we'll sell. We'll sell everything. Start over." Todd seemed really calm about it, maybe it was the pot.

"That's it?" she asked. "What about your art collection? The wine? The boat?"

"At least we have things to sell, don't we?"

"Don't you hear me? We're ruined. We have nothing," she cried. She was back to that girl in the trailer park.

Todd looked at her sideways, put his hands in his pockets. His linen trousers she'd bought from Rubinacci, the finest tailor in Milan, and they still fit him. Okay, so maybe he'd only gained ten pounds. It felt like fifty the way he moped around all year. "We have each other. That's not nothing," he said.

Ellie contemplated that. She remembered her earlier hysterics, the anxiety of seeing him flirt with a pretty young girl. She was forty years old now. How did it happen, how did she get so old? Yet he looked at her like she was still the babe in the braless tank top he'd met all those years ago, and she wasn't even that young then. When they met, she was already a mom, she'd already lived an entire life, many lives.

Everyone cheats, her mom told her. But her mom was wrong. Todd hadn't cheated. "You weren't having an affair," she said.

"And neither were you."

They both laughed out loud. It was cathartic. They used to laugh all the time.

"So? Are we good?" she asked.

"Actually, I have a confession to make," he said.

Oh god. He did cheat. He was a cheater. Ellie felt a stab in her heart. They wouldn't survive this, and they didn't have a prenup. She would never forgive him. But he wasn't talking about another woman. He was talking about another job offer.

"You know how I got laid off at the network?" he asked.

"Yeah," she said, her eyes narrowing.

"I wasn't exactly laid off."

She inched away from him. "Excuse me? You told everyone you were sacked. It was on Deadline!"

They'd let him go without a golden parachute either, not like all those assholes who were fired only to walk away with bazillions. She hadn't been paying a lot of attention to it—it was his career; she figured he could take care of it. But she had been surprised to find he was unemployed with nothing to show for it.

"I quit," he said. "I left. I was sick of it. I was sick of the whole thing. I couldn't do it anymore."

"You . . . quit?" she said. "You quit your job?" She stared at him. He hadn't been fired? He'd walked away on his own?

Todd shrugged. "It was never what I really wanted to do."

"But you were so good at it!" she said.

"Not really," he said. "Ratings were down. We couldn't compete with streaming. If I hadn't quit, they would have fired me anyway."

"You don't know that."

He shrugged again. "Who knows."

"So what do you want to do?" she asked.

"I don't know," he said. "Mostly kind of be there for the kids. I wasn't around for Sam as much. I want to be there for Giggy, and the twins."

"So if you quit on your own, why were you so depressed?"

Todd shook his head. "I don't know, okay? Life is fucking hard."

Life is hard. That was the fucking truth. Even if you had everything you ever wanted handed to you. She thought of those rich kids she'd gone to high school with; none of them were happy. And even if you earned everything you had, life was still hard.

"So, are you okay? Do you forgive me?" he asked humbly.

"For quitting?" she asked. "I don't know. I guess. At least you weren't cheating."

"On you?" he nuzzled her cheek. "Never."

She smiled against his cheek and sighed.

"Babe, you sure you're all right?"

"I don't know." She pulled away. "I was just thinking about my old friend. Remember, the one I told you about? My best friend in high school?"

He tapped his cheek, thinking. "You mean Mishon?"

"No," said Ellie. "Not her. Mishon and I were friends but not that close. My friend who had that thing with my dad, remember?" she said. Sometimes, she still felt like that poor kid from the wrong part of town. Todd had grown up poor too, but they hadn't been poor the way her family was poor. He'd been shocked when she told him about her dad being in jail, and how he'd died, and what he'd done.

Todd remembered. "Leo, right?" he said.

"Yeah, the one who died," she said.

"I know, you told me."

"She died on her birthday."

Todd nodded, and they were silent for a while.

"I feel bad she died," Ellie said. "I feel so guilty."

"Why?"

"Because I got to live, and she didn't. I got out of that stupid town, and she didn't. She didn't even get to do anything, or become anyone," said Ellie. "It's so sad. You know, today is her actual birthday. I've been thinking of her all day."

"Well, honey, it's no use feeling guilty. Guilt is a useless emotion."

"I guess."

"Come here," he said.

She rested her head against his shoulder and let him hold her. She was home. She couldn't wait until the party was over and all these guests finally went back to their hotel rooms at sunrise, so they could be alone, together, so they could finally have sex.

FORTY-THREE

Never Say Goodbye

October 28
Twenty-Four Years Ago
4:00 P.M.

L eo's funeral was huge. Almost everyone from the high school
  came. Teachers, students, the principal. It was so sad. Everyone cried. No one talked about how she was found or who was
found with her. Mish tried to hide in the back, but Brooks held
her hand and he took her to the front row, eyes straight ahead. He
didn't let anyone come near her, didn't let anyone let her feel
ashamed. She was allowed to grieve. She was thankful for that.

School was a blur. She'd gone, but she couldn't remember anything. She didn't even graduate; she would end up getting her
GED when she moved back to New York after leaving Archer.

Mish's family didn't want a funeral. Her mom didn't want one
and her dad didn't have many relatives; he was estranged from his
dad, and his mom had died years ago. They gave his body to sci-
ence, and afterward it would be cremated or buried in a mass
grave where they put people who had no family. While only Mish
knew the truth of what happened, her mom had an inkling of the

truth, and the two of them agreed it was better if they forgot this man was even related to them.

"You know, Lita and I were pregnant at the same time," Janet said. "And he'd dated her before me."

Mish shuddered. Had he known? Did Leo? Everyone always said they looked alike, and they always joked that they were sisters. But were they? She decided she never wanted to know and it was better if Leo never knew either.

She remembered the last conversation she had with Leo. It was in Stacey's house, right before they left the party. They were leaving Stacey's room when Leo turned around abruptly. "Wait! I almost forgot. Here, take this," she said, handing Mish a business card. It was a peace offering, a way to apologize for kissing Brooks, and it was the only thing she had to give. She didn't want her friend to be mad at her. She wanted to give Mish something back.

"What's this?" asked Mish.

"It's a number, this woman, she approached me at the mall the other day, but she said I had to lose weight first. It's for her modeling agency." Leo shrugged. "I mean, I don't know if she's legit or not, but it's worth a try, right?"

Mish narrowed her eyes suspiciously. "Okay, but why are you giving it to me?"

"You should call her. You look like me. Hell, you're even prettier. And skinnier."

"What about you?" asked Mish. "Are you going to call her?"

Leo sighed. Would she call? She had planned to, but she felt like a balloon, deflated. She didn't think she would. She didn't want to find out the offer wasn't real; it would kill too many dreams. "I don't know. Probably not. You call. Call for me," said Leo. "Promise?"

"Okay," said Mish. "I will." She put the card in her pocket. Leo knew Mish would call. Mish wasn't scared of anything. If it turned out to be a scam, Mish would just laugh, she wouldn't feel crushed. She would keep going, she would find a way out.

"Okay," said Leo. "Good."

"I love you," said Mish. "You're my best friend."

FORTY-FOUR

The Birthday Girl

October 20
The Present
1:00 A.M.

Michelle Cuzo de Florent-Stinson decided Mish was a stupid nickname. The woman at the modeling agency was the first person to call her by her full name, Michelle, so that most people she met through work or the fashion and advertising world called her Michelle, and then an affectionate roommate from New York called her Ellie, and it stuck. She'd gone by Ellie so long that when Mishon (formerly Shona) Silverstein came back to her life and asked to be called by her real name, she understood. Names reflected where you were in life, marked the people who knew you at certain phases. To her husband, she was Ellie; to Blake, *Elle* (because he thought it sounded better than "Ellie"); to Leo, she'd been Mish.

Leo, who died at sixteen. She never graduated from high school. She never left Portland. Never left Oregon.

If she'd lived, would Ellie even know her? Would they be friends or would she be one of those people she blocked on Facebook because they knew too much of her past?

Mish—and yes, sometimes she still thought of herself as Mish, especially when Leo came up—felt guilty.

This was the life Leo had dreamed about.

This was everything she'd ever wanted.

"What's up? You all right?" asked Todd. "Madison says we need to leave now or we'll miss the entire thing." They were standing in the middle of the hallway, in front of the pool doors; outside, the party was winding down, almost everyone had left.

"The night Leo died," she said. "You know how my dad died too?"

Todd nodded. "Murder-suicide or something, right? He killed her and then killed himself?"

"Not quite." She took a deep breath. She told him what she'd done. How she'd opened the door, how that moment had cost Leo her life. How her dad had shot Leo.

"I know," said Todd. "You told me this on our first date."

"Except that's not the whole story," she said. She told him the truth. About how her dad chased her, slipped and fell, and hit his head. How they didn't call the ambulance. How he came to, and how she grabbed the gun and pulled the trigger.

"I was so scared," she said. She was the one who'd done it. Maybe he would have bled out. Or maybe he would have survived. But she never gave him the chance. She made that decision for him.

"He was dead anyway," Todd said. "And you did the right thing. Even if it had gone to court, you would have been innocent. You have the right to self-defense."

"I guess," she said.

"Well, I don't guess, I *know*, and you know what else I know?" he asked gently.

"What?"

"It's your birthday."

"Technically, my birthday isn't till next week," Ellie reminded him.

"Right. But the party's tonight. So let's celebrate."

She shrugged. "We've been doing that all night."

"Yeah, and it's not over till the drag queen sings. We're not even at the first after-party yet, and it's almost time for the second."

She felt a small smile forming on her face. "Okay."

"Okay." He smiled, and he really was so handsome still, and she thought, no matter what, even with the ten extra pounds, she would always find him handsome, until they were old and toothless and drooling. Wasn't that worth more than all the money in the world?

The house was almost empty, so it was a surprise when the door opened and one last guest appeared. It was Harry Kim, her would-be investor.

"Happy birthday!" he said.

"Harry! What are you doing here? I thought you said you couldn't make it. I've been texting you all night, begging you not to leave me and telling you I need you, don't do this."

Todd raised his eyebrows. Mystery solved. Of course Ellie would only text so passionately to a business partner. It was classic Ellie.

"I was on a plane to come here," Harry said. "And you wouldn't let me finish explaining."

"Explain what?"

"The deal's off because we want to do a new deal. We don't want to just own fifty percent of Wild & West, we want to grow it. But there's a catch: We need to go down-market, sell to the off-brand stores. We have exclusives to Marshalls and Ross Dress for Less. We could make this a hundred-million-dollar business."

"What?"

"Yes, I had the new papers drawn up. But I didn't want to bother you on your birthday."

"Harry Kim!"

"Actually, it was Sanjay's idea," Harry said. "When I told him we were buying your company, he said we'd make a killing if we went this route."

Sanjay. Of course. Friends don't let friends go bankrupt. Sanjay was the one who had paid the ransom, after all, when she'd been kidnapped in Dubai.

She calculated the risks and benefits; she would be selling her clothes to bargain shoppers, to people who couldn't afford the good stuff but the facsimile. Then she realized, yes, she would do it—she would do it for the girl she used to be. So rich ladies in Boca would stop buying her outfits, she would stop being invited to Fashion Week, *Vanity Fair* wouldn't care about someone who sold clothes to the masses. To the poor.

But she wouldn't be broke.

In fact, if Harry was right, she'd be richer than she'd ever been. Todd raised his eyebrows. He'd done the same calculations too.

"Go, everyone's at the club," she said. "The party bus is still outside. Tell them to wait for us. I just have to grab my purse."

Ellie grabbed her purse and walked out of the Palm Springs house they would place on the market next month after Todd was diagnosed with dry-eye syndrome and could no longer be in the desert (Sterling would be so excited to flip it!), hand in hand with her husband to the waiting Uber to take them to the weeds-to-shithole restaurant her Parisian designer had retrofitted with more zhush.

She wasn't broke. She wouldn't have to file for bankruptcy. Her business would continue, and her family was intact. Her stepdaughter, hopefully, wouldn't be expelled from Stanford. But even if she was, who cared? There were other schools. And Ellie had never even gone to college, and look at where she was now.

Giggy at least had one good friend, and the twins—well, the twins were the twins.

Tomorrow she would craft a budget, tomorrow she would figure out a new financial plan, tomorrow she would start living within her means.

But that was tomorrow.

Today wasn't over yet.

Today was still her birthday.

Acknowledgments

Wow, I've wanted to write this book for more than a decade, right before we bought the house in Palm Springs, where I was supposed to have my fortieth birthday party. We never had the party, so I wrote the book instead, even though we've already sold the house. My husband, Mike Johnston, has heard about this book in so many permutations, mostly as this fantasy that I would be able to write it one day. "One day I will write my Palm Springs murder novel!" I vowed. Thanks, honey, for listening to every plot point and for cackling at every joke.

Thank you to my awesome editor, Jill Schwartzman, who believed and loved and encouraged this book. JILL!!! THANK YOU!!!

Thank you to Marya Pasciuto, Jamie Knapp, Elina Vaysbeyn, and everyone at Dutton!!!

Thank you to Richard Abate and Rachel Kim at 3 Arts Entertainment, who keep the lights on in all my houses. Thank you to Ellen Goldsmith-Vein and Eddie Gamara, who turn them into movies and TV shows. YOU GUYS ARE THE BEST!!!!

Thank you to my friends. There are so many! I am so incredibly blessed. Thank you to my NYC Gang, Spin Peeps, #beloveds text thread, Soho House lunch bunch, Il Pastaio squad, X-rated Xmas crew, Columbia pals, Tween Hangout parents, West Brooklyn Writers, PettyCashOGs, Kooorooon, and CoreQuadMoms. I love you guys. THANK YOU!!!! Book party!!!

Thank you to my family, who keeps me grounded and sane. DLCs Rule!!!!!!

Thank you to my kid, my favorite child, my one and only, my joy. As she would say (text): ILYSM!!!!!!!

Thanks for reading, and to all my readers, I believe this is my fiftieth book, so I am still younger than my book count. Thank you for reading my books for so long!!!!! Thank you for letting me write stories for a living.

—*Melissa de la Cruz,*
Los Angeles, March 2019